Letters From Elsewhere

Jacqui Greaves

Published by Jacqui Greaves, 2023.

LETTERS FROM ELSEWHERE

First edition. September 8, 2023.

ISBN: 979-8223934837

Written by Jacqui Greaves.

Table of Contents

This collection would never have emerged from the darkness without the unwaivering support of my fellow Tauranga Writers.

A special thanks to Lee, Carol and Annie.

A LETTER FROM ELSEWHERE

Exhibit # 5638-4662H: NOT TO BE COPIED OR REMOVED FROM THE ARCHIVES

• • • •

Dear [NAME REDACTED],

I'd never believed in alien abductions until it happened to me. Being taken wasn't glamorous or exciting, there were no bright lights or melodic messages like you see in the movies. I just woke from a bad night's sleep to find myself strapped onto a reclined metal frame.

As it turns out, people are abducted all the time. They're taken, probed and tested. Most are judged unacceptable and returned to their beds without any memory of the event. The unfortunate few who recall their experience are those who already suffer from some sort of brain disorder or damage. For them, the probes and tests just make their pre-existing conditions worse. It's an unavoidable side effect. The collectors do all they can for those poor souls, but their trauma is real and untreatable.

In my case, I endured the probes (some of which were, if I'm to be honest, very enjoyable). I passed all their tests. My scores on the self-preservation matrix were at the top-end of the scale. On that strength alone, I was offered a position as one of the elite forward scouts. In my post-probe, post-orgasmic bliss, I agreed. It seemed to offer a much more exciting future than being a bus driver on the narrow, and often unforgiving, roads of Wellington.

The company that recruited me were entrepreneurs. On their behalf, forward scouts travelled space and time dimensions in search of new worlds, new resources, new technologies and new opportunities the company could buy, sell, trade, market or otherwise exploit. I know what you're thinking. Why did they recruit me of all people? We humans think of ourselves as fragile creatures. That's a fallacy. We're tough and robust, but the characteristic most crucial to the company, the one they will pay above market rates to acquire, is our phenomenal will to live.

They chose me because I'm a fighter – a scrapper – a survivor. I didn't end up a bus driver because my life was a bunch of sweet-smelling roses. As you know all too well, casual violence, drug and alcohol abuse, and sexual predators featured through-out my youth and spilled into my early twenties. Petite blondes like us seldom escape the underbelly of the city unscathed, but I'd fought my way clear. Most of my friends got left behind, including you. I hope you remained on the streets. There were worse places to end up in the city than those streets.

Anyway, I signed the contract and joined the company. I received the obligatory identification tattoos on my right forearm, left shoulder and middle-lower back, and was issued with my custom-made set of uniforms. Each uniform for a specific class of planet and designed to mitigate the variable environmental conditions and challenges each presented to a human body. It took some weeks to learn how to put each uniform on, and how to use their various systems. Communication systems were pretty standard throughout, although some had more complicated translation modules than others. The most difficult thing to adapt to was movement in liquid and gaseous environments, along with their associated variable gravities. It was weird.

The first year in my new position was the absolute worst. In that year alone I survived wars, explosions, insectoid attacks, gases, and temperatures both too hot and too cold. It was rough going, and on more than one occasion I wished to be back in my bus, shuttling depressed workers between their pastel box-like suburban homes and their dead-end jobs in the city's skyscrapers. There are some terrifying things in the many universes, but none so dreadful as a life without meaning. Being a forward scout gave my life meaning. I had an important role in the company, and fortunes, including my own, were made and lost with my discoveries. That kept me going.

Over my career, I've survived love affairs, bites, toxins, attempted assassination, and mind-control. Being a forward scout gave me countless opportunities for sexual experiments far beyond what I could have imagined possible in my old life. I've been fucked with tentacles, plant pods, flagella and various other body parts by all manner of entities, including humanoids, robots and plants. The most surprising, was with a gaseous entity who satisfied me in ways nothing with a body has ever managed. I didn't even need to get out of my uniform for that one. But I never, ever got down to it with anything that looked like an insect. I've always hated insects.

All these years later I'm no longer the woman I was when they took me. The toes of my right foot froze solid when my boot got ripped off on an ice-bound moon that hailed diamonds. I lost a kidney to the spike of a sentient plant in a naked grapple to the death when it failed to understand that no meant no. On a planet with a three-week day, I was forced to cut off my left hand when I got trapped in a rock fall at the base of a cliff with a creeping, but steady incoming acid tide.

Those are physical costs, and to be honest, not that huge a deal. Body parts don't affect the self. The biggest sacrifice was to never see you, my friends and family, again. Given the nature of most of my relationships, I didn't care that much when I signed the contract, but over the years I've come to feel regret. Despite our mutual dislike of each other, I imagine my mother was concerned by my unexplained disappearance. I wonder if she mourned her youngest daughter at all? And you? Did you miss me?

Time hasn't been the same for me. It seems ridiculous to pine for people who have been dead for many years. I'm not even sure that you're still alive, or that climate change, famine or war hasn't destroyed humanity. By my reckoning I'm only forty-two. In theory still young enough to start a family. But I can't, not even with any of the other human scouts – the company made certain of that. Part of that orgasmic initial probing was my ovaries being replaced with artificial organs that produce modified hormones. Both menstruation and pregnancy were rendered impossible.

The urge to survive that's kept me going all this time is now all but gone. I've seen and experienced more than any human being should and fought my way back from the brink of death more times than I can remember. Through good commerce and astute trading, I've amassed a small fortune, which has enabled me to buy my independence from the company. With my remaining wealth, I've purchased a reconstructed left hand, my own purpose-built survival gear, a one-way fare to my destination, and the delivery of this message.

For my retirement, I've chosen a plant-based planet in a different universe from earth. The dominant intelligent entity on the planet is a large plant with rather delightful cones at the tip of hyper-mobile stems. They're a warm-sapped species with prehensile leaves. They're very affectionate, and yes, I do mean they fuck.

Humanoids are rare visitors to their planet but sought after in certain pockets of their society. The coating on the cones is psychotropic and results in orgasms that are extraordinary in their power and duration. In return, the dopamine humanoids release into their bloodstream when they orgasm are a powerful and addictive drug to the plants. The result is a mutually consuming symbiotic relationship, where the more we fuck the happier we both become. Until oblivion.

I don't expect to live long, which suits me just fine. I'm tired and all I want to do is fade away. But before I go, I'm looking forward to some well-earned, uninterrupted hedonistic pleasure and pure self-indulgence.

I suppose you're not alive to receive this message, but maybe it'll reach one of your relatives, or even offspring. I've sent it so someone knows that one of us reached beyond the stars and became more than she knew possible. I always wished the same for you.

With much love, always.

[NAME REDACTED]

Notes for Pastoral Researchers:

This letter was contained in a metallic tube found washed up on the shore of New Muscle Beach in the Independent State of California in the Twentieth Year Post-Schism. It was addressed to a city in New Zealand, which according to the Round Earth Legends was a small island state that existed on the lower hemisphere of the so-called globe.

This inflammatory and pornographic forgery has been included in our restricted archives to remind pastoral researchers and senators of the insidious lengths that the Blasphemers will go to in their endeavors to undermine the State Church.

It is well documented that the only aliens known to have existed were the now extinct species known as Mexicans. These highly invasive beings were exterminated during the Great Cleansing prior to the Schism. The records make no mention of them carrying out abductions, only of their invasions.

The remainder of the heresies contained in the document are pure fabrication. The idea of travel to other planets is preposterous, as is the concept of other intelligences. Pastoral science has proven the only intelligence is that given by God to his chosen zealots who live grace of His glory in this Independent State of California.

The final proof of the fantastical nature of this document is the suggestion that a woman is an autonomous being, divorced from her reproductive and domestic functions. Again, pastoral science has shown, with statistical certainty, that women possess little intelligence or self-awareness: their God-given purpose is to service men and reproduce.

END.

LA FOLLE

J e suis *la Folle du Roi*
        My name is Mathurine–*Mathurine la Folle*.
    I am the King's fool. Oh...but I am so much more than that.
    I am the woman to his man: he, the feminine to my masculine. I, the commoner to his royalty: he, the puritan to my whore. Without me his court is incomplete. Without him I am simply a mad woman.
    Where I come from the world is different. Slaves rule their masters, fish live in trees and men bear children. Finding myself here, in this reversed world, has quite excited my mind. I am never sure at which point my madness transforms from pathological to synthetic for the distraction of my beloved Henry – *Mon Roi*.
    As *Mathurine la Folle* I carry the King's power. I use my words to cut, mortify, distract and assuage. Treasonous blasphemies and burlesque truths slide from my smiling lips. Excused of my gender I navigate the treachery and intricacies of every royal hallway. I am all-seeing and all-hearing; not a single humiliation or vulgarity escapes my attention. I know the secrets, fears, perversions and terrors of the Court.
    Tonight, I dine at his table. He has expectations of me, and I never disappoint. I adjust my armour and ensure the sword I wear hangs at the correct angle. The long folds of my robes hide the split that runs from hem to hip. I stare into the eyes of the short-haired Amazonian in the looking glass. She glares back with eyes that glow feverishly in the candlelight.
    Dinner conversation flows like quicksilver, rolling around the table, breaking apart then re-merging. The topics leap; war, economics, salt tax, sex, religion, politics. My tongue is sharp, my mind sharper. Few can counter my parries. Mad I may be, but I am a fool only by appointment.

The syphilitic man of medicine opines on the filthy nature of women. I commiserate with him, for his very own mother was a case in point. I raise my voice so all at the table are aware of his error in choosing to exit his mother's cunny facing the wrong way. If only she'd had the benefit of a cloth his newborn face would not have been smeared with her shit. His adult face turns an unusual shade of purple as his mouth flaps in the way of a fresh caught fish lying on the banks of the River Seine.

The King barks with laughter, happy with my work. My King, I am, and always will be, your fool. *Toujours votre folle.*

While he may be my earthly master, at heart I am the instrument of the Virgin Mary. Never more so than when it comes to the conversion of damned Protestants. Any pleasure I gain in their conversion is my reward for good travails. She is pleased and rewards me often and in full.

Seated between two filthy Huguenots, I begin my work on their conversion. He to my left I permit entry to my inner self. I guide his hand between the folds of my robe. He dabbles his digits in my cleft. Concentrating on his task, the tip of his tongue protrudes and his eyes bulge.

His confrere to my right is treated to the ministrations of my strong and expert fingers. He swells with pleasure and his cheeks take on a ruddiness that cannot be explained by wine alone. As with all venereal disease, the pair will contract Catholicism through their inability to refuse what they are offered. I will pluck their souls at my leisure.

I regard my King. My love for him is without condition. Yet, I fear for his soul. As Henry of Navarre, he was a filthy protestant, proselytizing to take the Crown. The Virgin Mother has no concern for the manner of conversion, and I do not doubt her wisdom. My fear stems from his continued sympathies towards the Huguenots. I fear he will lapse–it is for me to assure his soul.

As his fool, my access to the King's chambers is unfettered. *Mathurine la Folle* poses no threat to the regent. But I am also Mathurine de Valois, unwavering servant of *Notre Dame*.

Within his inner sanctum, I have no need for disguise. We have danced this dance many times before. Tonight, I burn with rhapsodic fervour as the genderless fool is folded and set aside. I stand before my King as God has created me. Breasts, loosened from their armour, sway like hypnotic church bells.

The King falls to his knees to lick my toes in adoration. I welcome Henry to my mirror world–he enters willingly, without suspicion. Here, my King is my slave. He begs for my audience, my indulgence and my attentions. I feed him titbits, as I would any dog that simpers at my feet.

At my whim he is permitted to nuzzle, knead and stroke, but he must earn each privilege. Transgressions are punished with swift pain. He craves the mortification. His tongue laps at my living altar until Mother Mary rewards my commitment to his soul. He drinks of my wine and eats of my flesh. To complete his confirmation, I sheath his sword of flesh and receive his alms. My King is reborn. The mirror world dissolves–back here it is I that kneel at his feet.

Filled with his righteousness, I don my disguise and leave my King to his dreams. I stalk the halls in search of my dinner companions. My evening's work is incomplete.

Je suis Mathurine, la Folle du Roi.

I was mad and then healed–but not entirely.

THE MEMO

M EMORANDUM
TO: The Board
FROM: Diana D'olympus: CEO, Goddess Global Biomedicals
Ltd (GGBL)
SUBJECT: Implementation of Project Artemis
DATE: 30 April 2025
CC: Shareholders

• • • •

I announce the successful implementation of Project Artemis with immense pride.

As you are aware this project has been the company's sole focus ever since I took up my position fifty years ago. It has been our most ambitious and expensive investment both financially and in terms of personnel.

Thank you all for your support and forbearance over the years. I know the lack of information and reporting on Artemis has caused many of you great frustration. So, it is my absolute pleasure to provide some clarity on aspects of the project which have until now been too sensitive to share.

While some of what you read below may cause you confusion and distress, I urge you to read it through twice before you consider responding.

• • • •

STATED PROJECT GOAL:
Save the planet through applied biomedical solutions.

An ambitious goal that granted GGBL, and me as the CEO, a wide remit for research and application.

• • • •

BACKGROUND:

Project Artemis was established in 1975, in the context of a looming planet-wide ecological disaster.

At the time, there was an imminent threat of nuclear war, with a rapidly growing nuclear arsenal. The exponential increase in animal and plant extinctions was well established, and the growth rate of the human population was near its historical peak.

Since the project's inception, the global situation has only worsened. Global warming and the concomitant climate change have emerged as greater challenges to survival than nuclear war ever posed. Despite the wealth of scientific information urging the need for immediate attention, politicians have refused to act, and in many cases lobbied and voted against the planet's interests, making decisions based on short-term financial gains and political expediencies.

These human inadequacies may have doomed the planet, and I can only hope that the belated solutions provided by Project Artemis can immediately halt and begin to reverse the damage done.

• • • •

ASSUMPTIONS:

As GGBL Board members and Shareholders, you made a number of assumptions with regards to the project and failed in your due diligence and duties on numerous occasions.

1. You, without exception, interpreted the aim of the project as saving humanity.
2. You assumed I was who I said I was on my C.V. and never questioned how I could stay in the same position for half a century.
3. You expected to gain some financial reward for your role, speaking often of monetization while lacking even a basic

understanding of the true nature of Project Artemis.

· · · ·

ACTUAL GOAL OF PROJECT ARTEMIS:

To reduce the human population to levels that no longer cause any threat to the environment. It should be noted that level may be as low as a zero population.

Obviously, the greatest challenge has been to devise a biomedical mechanism that is easy to disperse and targeted only to human DNA. Given the close relationship between humans and primates (humans share 99% of their DNA with chimpanzees and bonobos, and 98% with gorillas) this took considerable time and resources.

Research teams were broken down into independent units, each investigating a single aspect of the Project. By locating each team in different institutions worldwide, they were unaware of the existence of each other. Private funding allowed GGBL to retain intellectual property over all discoveries and prevent the usual scientific peer review process through publication.

Production and dissemination of Artemis was achieved in the same manner. While I'm sure you'd like to know what Artemis is and does, that knowledge is irrelevant at this point. Just be assured it is efficient, 100% effective, fast and painless.

There are small pockets of uncontacted humans, who by way of their isolation may remain immune to Artemis. I wish them well and hope they continue to live their lives in harmony with nature, ignorant of the demise of their destructive cousins.

· · · ·

MY ACTUAL IDENTITY:

This is the point where most of you will be tempted to cease reading and dismiss this missive as the ramblings of a mad woman. I assure you they are not, as I am not a woman. To be specific, I am not a human woman. I concede, I may be somewhat mad, but that will happen to any immortal forced to live forgotten and ignored amongst the filth and greed of the mortal world.

I've had many titles and names over the ages, none of which I chose myself. Lady of the Beasts, Goddess of the Hunt, Goddess of the Wilderness, the Virgin Goddess, Goddess of Women, Midwife, Cynthia, Diana, and Artemis. I am all of them and more.

It never ceases to amuse me that my refusal to fuck or marry men lead to the Virgin Goddess moniker. Male historians have been notorious for their lack of imagination. Every single woman member of the Board will attest to my healthy sexual interest, I thank you all for those brief moments of delight. They were joyful sparks in the last of several thousand years of existence.

But I digress.

It's the titles Lady of the Beast and Goddess of the Hunt and Wilderness that should capture your attention. You've all admired my vast collection of bows, arrows and quivers, and yet never enquired as to my personal interest, nor questioned my likeness to the many sculptures and paintings of the Huntress that adorn the GGBL headquarters.

In times past I destroyed Kingdoms and spread plagues amongst those who failed to respect the creatures and places under my protection. Back then I was strong, feared, respected and worshipped. But as the ages passed, I slid from your minds. You left me weakened and the old ways became irrelevant. So, I've been forced to use other means. Which brings me back to Project Artemis.

· · · ·

IMPLEMENTATION OF PROJECT ARTEMIS:

I would like to assure you that SARS-CoV-2 (Covid 19) was not part of Project Artemis. It did, however, provide valuable data to assist with implementation.

Project Artemis was launched on 23rd April 2025. It is expected to be complete by 31 May 2025 with a small margin of error.

The method of dissemination is protected by numerous copyrights and the IP is held by me.

There is no cure or remedial action available.

• • • •

RECOMMENDATIONS:

I recommend you:

1. Accept your imminent demise with grace and dignity.
2. Keep the contents of this Memo confidential to avoid panic in the general population.
3. Spend your remaining 5 – 10 days with your loved ones.
4. Congratulate yourself on being at the forefront of saving the planet.

END.

PLEASE SIGN THE WAIVER

Dear Mums,
       I've arrived safely in Tauranga. The trip to the Zealandia Bubble was much longer than I'd imagined, but wow, so worth it!

I put on my new glasses before we landed at Tamaki Makaurau. It was amazing to see the colours, the green is incredible and the sea so blue. Nothing like what we're used to. The other kids were jealous they couldn't see as well as me.

Before we disembarked the attendants sprayed something to kill any bugs we might be carrying. They're very strong on biosecurity here. And, of course, we had to put on our masks.

Border control was a bit frightening. We had to fill in so many declarations and waivers. I'm so glad we'd downloaded them at home and practiced before I came. It saved a lot of time, but don't worry, I did what you told me and read every question twice. A couple of the kids must have filled the forms in wrong. They were taken away, and we haven't seen them since. I'm sure it was just a misunderstanding, and they'll turn up in time for our first excursion tomorrow.

Once we were all through border control, we collected our bags, and even though they'd been checked on departure, they were all put through the scanner again to make sure none of us had smuggled in anything illegal. Even though I knew I hadn't done anything wrong, I was really nervous. The biosecurity officers are so intimidating!

I'm so glad the testing and quarantining is no longer required on landing here. It would be so frustrating to be so close and have to sit in a room waiting for two weeks before you could go out. As it is, by the time we were escorted onto the shuttle it was almost dark. I was disappointed I couldn't see the countryside, but I guess we've got five days to enjoy the sights.

Our accommodation seems nice, and the sleeping quarters look really comfortable. Only two others are sharing with me tonight, apparently our fourth was one of the ones who didn't fill in their forms correctly or something.

I'm quite tired after the long trip, so I'll sign off now.

Love you both.

Your most adventurous offspring.

• • • •

Dear Mums,

Today was Ay-May-Zing!!!

The first news is that the two kids who didn't get through border control never turned up. The rumour going around is that they're animal rights activists, and well you know what that means! How do you think they passed the vetting process to come on the trip? Anyway, I guess it's lucky they got picked up at the border and didn't ruin our trip by doing something stupid in the middle of it.

But, back to the fun stuff...

Breakfast was the usual. I was kind of hoping they'd have some local dishes to taste, but I guess they just want us to eat and get going in the mornings. As it is, it takes us ages to get dressed and make sure our masks are on right. They've set up a buddy system to make sure we don't muck it up. Because we're missing a member of our group, we're a threesome, so two check one. That means I'm twice as safe, so you don't need to worry about me.

Our first activity was to climb Mauao, a lava dome that sits at the tip of a peninsular and guards the entrance to Tauranga Harbour. In colonial times, they called it The Mount – imagine being so unimaginative! It's 232m high, so a pretty strenuous climb, especially with our suits and masks on, but so worth the effort.

The trail winds up the side through a forest of native trees. I'd never seen anything like it. The pictures we looked at together before I left don't give you any idea of how beautiful they are up close. Some of the trunks are so old they're all twisted and gnarled. And, because we're visiting in summer, the pohutakawa trees are just covered in red flowers. It's so pretty it hurt my eyes, even with my glasses on!

Some of the kids struggled with the light and colours. It's so intense it made them feel a bit sick. They had to sit with their eyes shut for a while, because vomiting with your mask on is a real problem.

From the top of Mauao we could see all of Tauranga Moana. It's boundaried by the Pacific Ocean on one side and the Kaimai Ranges on the other. The harbour is enormous, with amoeba-like extrusions that push into the land creating a series of peninsulas and bays. There are also some islands. One of them, Matakana, sits opposite Mauao and extends away into the mists.

In the other direction is the open ocean. There's so much water. It's terrifying and thrilling all at once! There are a few islands out there too, some of them are reserves and can only be visited with a special permit. They seem to float and shimmer in the sun. Mesmerising.

And guess what else we saw? I know you can't, so I'll just tell you. CLOUDS! Yep, real clouds, made of droplets of water clumped together and suspended in the sky like magic. The ones we saw were the little fluffy ones. If you stared at them for long enough, you could see shapes and figures in them. I took some photos that I'll attach for you to show all my grandmas.

One of the group got so excited trying to take a selfie with a cloud, they stepped backwards too far and fell off a rock. It was a bummer, because they tore their suit and, despite getting a patch on it pretty quick, had to get medevacked back home. Despite that, and even though they told us not to, some of us raced down the steps. What a rush!

At the base of Mauao, they showed us the famous hotpools. The pools are filled with salt water heated by the earth. I know it's hard to imagine such a thing. Even though the volcano is dormant, the magma remains close enough to the surface to heat water. This is truly a dangerous land! None of us had our swimming suits with us, but even if we did, I'm not sure any of us have the gumption to sit in hot salt water.

After a standard lunch back at our accommodation, we got to paddle a real wooden canoe, or waka, in the harbour. This was a special treat, and only possible because there was no wind. The water was as smooth as the skin on your beautiful faces. According to our guides, if the water surface is rough then we could suffer from what they call 'sea sickness', which can result in vomiting. And, like I said before, vomiting and masks really don't go together! We had to wear special buoyancy devices that would keep us afloat if the worst happened and we fell overboard.

This was our first chance to try to spot some of the local marine wildlife. Before we'd even left the pontoon, we could see jellyfish pulsing their way along just below the surface. One of the guides tossed a handful of something into the water and a fleet of small silver fish shot up from the depths to fight over the tiny morsels. Just beautiful. I tried to get a photo for you, but they move so fast it came out blurry. It'll give you an idea though and although it's not as good as the pictures we looked at in the brochures, you know I took this one and saw it for myself, with my very own eyes and glasses.

Paddling the waka was such a buzz. The guides showed us how to hold the paddle and make it pull us through the water, no engines, only our limbs to propel ourselves. We each had a paddle and sat in pairs, paddling on our own side. No matter how careful we were, water got splashed around. At first it was scary, but once we realized it couldn't touch us, we relaxed and began to enjoy ourselves.

We had a couple of real treats. First, we saw a korora, or little blue penguin. Imagine it! A bird that flies in the water! Crazy! It didn't seem too bothered by us and swam around next to our waka for a while before diving out of view. Then, a few minutes later, one of the guides spotted a fur seal lounging on the rocks. It was so well camouflaged;

we only saw it when it lifted its head to look at us. Such an amazing creature. A mammal, more comfortable in the water than on the land.

I reckon our suit manufacturers could learn a thing or two from the feathers of the penguin and the pelt of the fur seal. Both are designed to protect the animals from the wet and cold, and work remarkably well! I quite fancy myself in an imitation penguin feather suit, all sleek in blue and white!

Unfortunately, a few ripples started to disturb the sea, so the rest of our paddle was cut short. By the time we got back to the jetty, some of the group were feeling quite unwell (yes, the same ones that had to shut their eyes on the climb up Mauao – losers!).

That was all our activities for today. Dinner was the usual. I'd really hoped they'd offer us a little taste of something a bit exotic, this is the Extreme Aqua Adventure Tour after all, but no. Maybe tomorrow?

Anyway Mums, I hope you enjoy the photos.

Love you,

Your most adventurous offspring.

• • • •

Dear Mums,

So, our group got a little bit smaller again today. I guess that's why we had to sign all those waivers – haha! But I'm getting ahead of myself...

While eating our boring breakfast we had an actual earthquake!! It wasn't a big one, but enough that everything shook for a bit. Some of the kids dived to the floor and into doorways. I didn't, because I really wanted to experience it! I can't describe how it made me feel. Even though it was small, it really highlighted to me the raw and dangerous nature of this land and planet. Afterwards, the guides told us we were super lucky to have felt one on such a short trip.

The earthquake rattled some of the kids. One decided to go home and left straight away. Another four decided not to participate in today's activities. Their loss!

Today, was our Salt-Water Submersion Experience. I'm sure you've been looking at my itinerary so know that in the morning we had the Extreme Beach Activity, and then this afternoon the Death-Defying Dive. Let me tell you, both activities were even better than how they were described in the brochure!

We had to put on special swimming suits. One of the most dangerous things at the beach (apart from the water of course) is sand. It's made up of tiny little grains, mostly of crushed up volcanic rocks, but some of it is crushed up bits of shells...yes, the shells of living animals...crazy huh? Anyway, because the grains are so small, they risk getting caught in our usual suits where they can rub and weaken the material. The swimming suits are extra smooth and thick, but even more uncomfortable to wear.

It's really hard to walk on the sand, too. We had to practice for ages before getting it right. To get forward momentum, you kind of have to dig in then push forward. It was really tiring to start with but gets easier once you get used to it. The closer you get to the water the firmer the sand gets, so the trick is to get close to the water then stay there! Of course, once you're near the water you have to keep an eye out for rogue waves.

The ocean is never still, waves are constantly rolling in. The sea rises and rises in long lines until gravity takes over and water at the top is pulled down. Because of the forward motion, the water forms a foaming curl. It crashes down and rushes up across the sand before getting sucked back out to sea again. Sometimes, one of the waves is bigger that the rest, or two waves merge together and the water surges higher up the beach. If you don't watch out, you can be knocked down by the force of the water and dragged out into the sea.

I've listened to recordings of the sound the waves make and it's such a shame that our suits mean we can't hear it in real time. I'd love to hear that thunderous crashing and wooshing while standing on an actual beach.

I found the patterns left in the sand fascinating. The grains of sand are different colours, sizes and weights, so the water moves them in different ways. When the waves retreat, new geometric patterns are left behind. The patterns change with each wave. The colour patterns are harder to see in the drier sand further up the beach. There, the wind moves the lighter grains of sand and creates ridges and mounds around larger, heavier objects like washed up shells, wood, and clumps of seaweed.

On some parts of the beach, the sand is replaced by piles and piles of shells. Even through the protective suit, I could feel them crunch as I moved over them. They're so beautiful. It's really tempting to try to tuck a couple of them away to keep as souvenirs, but our suits have no pouches and it's totally forbidden, of course!

We followed our guides along the waters-edge to the rocks and pools at the base of Mauao. The rockpools vary in size from smaller than one of my back feet, to large enough for several of us to climb into. The larger the rockpool, the more life contained in it. Some of the bigger ones even had small fish flitting amongst the seaweeds.

We came to a beach of shells where the sea was surrounded by rocks. The water was calm and protected from waves. This was where we did our first water submersion. I wasn't the first chosen to follow a guide into the water and it was super frustrating to watch others go halfway in then lose their nerve and flounder back to the dry beach of shells. But mothers, I'm proud to say that I was the first to go all the way in!

The suits block all sensation of cold or pressure, so I'm not sure what stopped the others. I was careful to follow the guide's instructions and set my suit to negative buoyancy so all my feet would stay on a solid surface. I just kept on walking until I was completely submerged. It was like entering another world all over again. Instead of trees and birds, this world was filled with seaweeds and fishes. Once we were deep enough, the guide adjusted our suits to neutral buoyancy and for a moment we floated with the movement of the water. It was magical.

All too soon my time was up, and I was back in the air, crunching my way up the shelly beach. Only about two-thirds of the group were brave enough to fully submerge. Those of us who did, agreed it was a life-changing moment. The ones that didn't were sullen over lunch. It meant they didn't get to go on the afternoon Death-Defying Dive. They did get a chance to try the full submersion experience again, but only a few of them managed it. I feel sad for the ones that didn't. Most of them left before dinner.

This afternoon was crazy! And I can't believe how patient I've been not telling you about it first! I hope you haven't cheated and read ahead already!

So here it goes...

Those of us allowed to participate in the Death-Defying Dive were taken to the pontoons in the harbour again. There, we boarded a boat with an engine that sped us across the surface of the ocean. Even though we were in our swimsuits, we still had to wear flotation devices in case we fell overboard, and just as well! We hit our first big wave in the entrance to the harbour between Mauao and Matakana Island. It's a narrow channel and the ocean water was rushing in against the wind. Our guide told us this was perfect conditions for standing waves and to hold on tight. Not everyone did and two kids fell out. We didn't stop for them. According to the guide, a chase boat picked them up.

I felt a bit guilty seeing them getting smaller and smaller as we sped away. They missed out on the absolute best activity and, later, we were told they were sent home for not following instructions. It seems a bit strict, but rules are rules, I guess!

I can't describe to you the feeling of being in a small primitive watercraft, skidding across the surface of an open ocean. So much water with the thinnest of shells keeping us afloat. It's a bit like what I imagine a spacewalk would be like. A fragile being in an environment that would kill you if you weren't enclosed in a protective suit.

We skirted around Mauao, past the beach we'd walked along this morning, around Moturiki Island and on to Motuotau Island. The boat stopped not far offshore from the island, in 'shallow' water. The island is small and very close to the beach. It's covered in trees, and although we could see lots of birds, we of course couldn't hear them. They told us lots of penguins nested on the island, but the parents swim out to sea to feed during the day, so we didn't see any.

The island protected us from the wind and the surface of the water was calm. The few of us left are the hardy ones and none of us suffered from sea sickness. We didn't stay on the boat for long. The guides reminded us of the main safety rules and then lowered the ladder.

We had to descend one at a time. This time I was the first! You'd be so proud of me. I didn't hesitate at all. I set my suit to negative buoyancy, took a good grip on the ladder and lowered myself into the water until I was submerged. At the bottom of the ladder, I was given the all-clear to let go. As we'd been instructed, I pushed off a little and sank to the sea floor.

I landed on a rock and slid off sideways into a forest of seaweed. Some of my limbs got tangled in the weed. For a moment I panicked a bit because I couldn't tell which way was up and which way was down, but the suit did its work and got me upright again. By the time the next kid floated down beside me, I was all sorted. Whew!

Then I realized I was surrounded by fish. When I'd slid off the rock, I'd crushed some kina (those greenish spiky things we laughed at in the brochures) and the fish were going crazy. They flashed all silver and blue as they rushed in to eat the flesh out of the shells. It was gross and amazing!

By the time the feeding frenzy was over, all my fellow adventurers were on the sea floor with me. We watched the hull of the boat as it zoomed away, leaving a trail of silver bubbles in its wake. Our death-defying challenge was to follow our guide to the safety of the beach. And Mums, trust me, that was easier said than done!

Visibility underwater is way, way less than on land, and the wind had stirred up the sediment, so it was even less than usual. Add to that the multitude of distractions all around us, and it didn't take long for the group to get separated. For a moment, I was all alone.

Something incredible happened when I was on my own. I saw a real live shark. Not up close, thank goodness, but in the distance. It was a dark shape cruising through the water, moving with the ease of an interstellar cruiser. No one believes me here, but I know what I saw!

Despite seeing the shark, I didn't panic, I just kept moving in the direction I'd last seen the guide. The seafloor was rising, so I was sure I was heading in the right direction. As soon as I felt the surge of the waves, I knew I'd be safe. I set my swimsuit to positive buoyancy and let the waves surf me into the shallows.

Honestly Mums, if I die in my sleep tonight it will have all been worth it! Not that I think I'll sleep tonight because I'm still fizzing from everything I achieved today. At least I won't keep anyone awake, I've got the room to myself tonight as I've been told my two buddies elected to go home. Seems a bit odd as they were both really good adventurers, but I guess you just never know.

Love as always,

Your bravest offspring.

• • • •

Dear Mums,

I guess anything was going to be an anti-climax after yesterday, but today was just the worst. It's impossible to tell you how the day made me feel, so all I'll do is tell you where we went and what we did. I can't tell you everything because of the waivers I signed, but I'm pretty sure you'll understand what I mean.

This morning, they announced we'd be having a different day than planned. We were meant to go white-water rafting down a river in the Kaimai Ranges, which as you know I was pretty excited about! Instead, because our numbers are now so few, they'd got permission for us to go to one of the few wildlife sanctuaries not on an offshore island.

Of course, we had to sign more waivers and bunch of other forms before travelling to the Matua peninsular. There's a huge biosecurity fence erected around the entire peninsular, with double gates to ensure nothing gets in, or out, without permission. The guards here make the ones at the border look friendly!

As soon as we entered, we saw our very first humans. To be honest, they didn't look half as scary as I thought they'd be. They're mammals, of course, with only four limbs, two of which they use for locomotion. The way they walk looks very unwieldy and unsteady, and I've got no idea how they hold their heads up on those spindly necks of theirs! The other pair of limbs seem to be mainly for grasping things, although I got the impression they were also involved in communication. Our guide told us there were several races of humans held at this facility. To be honest, I couldn't tell them apart, they all looked the same to me.

We were allowed to enter their shelters, little boxes made of wood and sometimes stone – very primitive. Compared to us, the conditions they live in are squalid, I'm not sure the authorities are really taking care of them. They all seem broken and compared to the pictures of wild humans I've seen, these ones looked underfed.

Having seen these pathetic remnants of a species, it's hard to believe they almost destroyed their beautiful jewel of a planet. I'm glad the authorities decided to protect a few of them, after all, humans are also an integral component of the biodiversity of Earth. What does upset me though, is the way they are treated. Humans are obviously sentient, and yet we force them to live like savages.

The visit left me quite upset and I have a lot to think about. As you know I've never understood the animal rights movement, but todays visit has left me with some new thoughts on the matter.

This trip has changed me in so many ways. I thought I'd led a good life before I had these experiences. Now, I'm not so sure. I don't know what to do.

I love you all so very much,
Your blessed offspring.

• • • •

NOTICE OF DEATH

To: Mothers of individual DD5678FX4

Please be advised that your offspring suffered a fatal accident whilst visiting the planet Earth. They entered a restricted area without permission and while attempting to interfere with the local wildlife, their hazmat suit was damaged. They did not survive exposure to the toxic element 'oxygen' contained in Earth's atmosphere.

As per all waivers signed by your offspring and yourselves, there will be no financial reimbursement for your loss.

Our sympathies to your entire colony.

-END NOTICE-

FLOWER GIRL

When her husband-to-be found her, she was simply known as Sing Song Girl No. 27. She was languishing in a Flower Ship, providing recreation and sensuality to those who could afford her. The Flower Ships appeared derelict, rusting hulks floating against the ancient space-dock at the edge of the Pearl Reflection Nebula in the Kardon Quadrant. It was only on entry, for a hefty fee, that visitors were able to appreciate the ships' true beauty. No expense was spared on their interior decoration, ensuring not only a discreet visit, but one of great luxury and comfort.

Raised in service, Sing Song Girl No. 27 had not so much learned her craft as absorbed it through daily exposure. Dressed in a figure-hugging red gown, made from the finest Mausian spider silk, she danced with swaying hips and sang for her clients before kneeling at their feet to wrap her red-stained lips around their cocks. Her skill was legendary.

To come in her mouth was described as surpassing the pleasure of witnessing the birth of a star.

How Zhamon came to hear of her she never knew. As one of the most feared pirates to ever take to the stars, he seldom allowed himself to be put in a position of vulnerability. To avoid the need to visit women, he had pressed into his service Posai, the son of an indebted trader. The boy's downy face and pursed lips had caught Zhamon's attention and Posai became a cabin-boy in all senses of the word. He had yielded to his charismatic leader with such enthusiasm that, in reward, Zhamon adopted him as a son.

But when Sing Song Girl No. 27 knelt at Zhamon's feet, he was lost to her charms. His desire so great, he abducted her from the Flower Ship. His obsession for her only grew when she tried to kill him. To mollify her, he proposed marriage.

Being a young woman of grand ambition, Sing Song Girl No. 27 recognised an opportunity. The stars had glittered in her obsidian eyes since she'd stepped aboard Zhamon's flagship. She refused his marriage proposal and withdrew her services until he agreed to share his profits and his leadership.

The arrangement worked better than either had imagined. Their business flourished under her influence. Her beauty, grace and charms were undisputed – but what no one expected was her iron will, military genius and lust for battle. Working together, their reputation grew, and the fears of the authorities sharpened.

She was saddened at Zhamon's death, a few short imperial years after their marriage, but he had been foolish taking his ship so close to a solar storm. She had little sympathy for fools. Still, out of respect for the man who had opened the universe to her, she changed her name to Shasm-Zha, the Widow of Zhamon.

Contrary to expectations, Shasm-Zha did not forfeit her position as the head of the Red Banner Fleet, and the captains of the flotilla rallied to her. To further consolidate her position, Shasm-Zha married her stepson, the ever-accommodating Posai. As an unexpected bonus, the marriage of convenience was also sexually gratifying.

In the first weeks of their marriage, the couple discovered delights denied them in the service of Zhamon. Posai's mouth was almost as masterful as Shasm-Zha's and, for the first time, she understood the pleasure that made an exploding starship seem unimpressive. The look of bliss on her young husband's face each time he explored her hidden space urged her to reward him with more vigour.

• • • •

To the Emperor of the Gerentage Supercluster, Shasm-Zha's rise in power was incomprehensible.

As patron of the Flower Ships, the Emperor was afforded first rights to plunder the Flower Girls' virginity when they came of age.

Despite using his privilege often, he was fussy. He had considered Sing Song Girl No. 27 a special treat. Not only for her tight pussy, which had offered just the right amount of resistance to his initial incursion, but also for her red-stained lips and the tricks she could perform with her lacquered fingernails.

He still recalled the sensation of her sharp nail sliding into his arse – a sweet agony in contrast to her velvet tongue on his balls. He'd had to hold his paunch aside to watch her lips on his cock. When she'd twisted her nail, his hips had twitched, thrusting his tiny dick into her mouth along with a premature load of imperial seed. She'd swallowed, all the while staring up at him with unblinking black eyes.

Now, she was fucking him in an entirely different fashion.

Her flotilla had swelled to over 1,700 ships. They attacked any trading vessels attempting to enter or leave the Kardon Quadrant. Whether weapons, platinum, diamonds or dark matter fuel, Shasm-Zha controlled this corner of his empire and his every attempt to fight back had resulted in defeat. Not only had the former Flower Girl managed to effect organisation with her Pirate Code but, in exchange for protection, she'd commandeered entire farming planets for her Red Banner Fleet.

In desperation, and with a great loss of face, the Emperor had been forced to call for support from his trading partners: the twin royals King Stephen and Queen Matilda of the Brittania Galaxy; the Grand Pensionary Pieter van de Spiegel of the Batavian Cluster; and, most galling of all, mad Queen Maria XI of the far-flung Arberian Supercluster. They were now gathered in his Palace war room, along with the Empress, to witness the defeat of the pirates. Their combined naval fleets were assembled, and Shasm-Zha's Red Banner Fleet was blockaded with no hope of escape from the might of the intergalactic Potentatial forces.

• • • •

Shasma-Zha stood alone on the bridge of her command ship. The Red Banner Fleet had come together for their periodic conclave, during which grievances were aired, judgements were made, and Shasm-Zha distributed the Fleet's earnings amongst her almost 2,000 Captains. They had met in the usual place at the outer rim of the Bingdilian black holes, a twin system, which struck terror into the hearts of all but the most skilled of navigators. The naval blockade had trapped them between the twins and the Shadax Dark Nebula running through the Joali Constellation. The Red Banner Fleet's only egress was through the Potentatial force.

With a smile, she recalled her very first victory over an Imperial naval vessel. She'd given the crew the option of an honourable death, or life under her command. Rigid adherence to their customs dictated the officers' choice. They were decapitated – their bodies ejected from one airlock and their heads from another. But most of the crew didn't care who they served and had switched sides without a second thought.

She and Posai had embraced in victory on the bridge of the conquered Star-Frigate. His erection had stabbed into her hip. It was all the prompting she'd needed to drop her silk trousers and bend over the main command consul. Posai had fucked her hard, leaving bruises on her hips. It had been incredible, both of them grunting and shouting profanities as they orgasmed.

After her second victory, Shasm-Zha had used a thruster lever as a dildo while Posai sat in the Commander's chair and jerked himself off. In time they craved an audience and, before lopping off the officers' heads, forced them to witness the sexual violation of their vessel of war. Innumerous victories later, nothing excited the couple more than fucking in the still-warm blood of their foes, surrounded by severed heads observing through dead eyes.

They were fond memories, but this was not the time to dwell on them. The pirate leader turned to stare at the Potentatial naval force on her holographic display. Based on the imagery, she calculated the strengths and weaknesses of her opponents. As she made her final assessment, a spark of lust shimmied through her body. Once again, the tiny-dicked Emperor had shot his load too soon.

Shasm-Zha had learned the power of subterfuge during her time on the Flower Ships. To the lazy observer, her vessels were filthy, rundown and obsolete. But the rust, pockmarks and crusty patches were mere paintings on hulls of smooth titanium alloy, reinforced with chromium steel. The pirate ships were laden with weapons hidden within covered recesses, but the greatest treasures were held within.

State-of-the-art guidance and navigation systems had been installed into every vessel, but the pirate's unique strength was their boarding system. It enabled the crew's holographic doppelgängers to penetrate enemy vessels with real swords, wreaking real havoc, while the pirates themselves stayed on their own vessels in total safety.

Shasm-Zha launched her attack.

The stories of the overwhelming destruction of the Potentatial Navy went on to spawn children's nightmares for hundreds of years. Parents threatened their offspring with a visit from the Queen of Pirates if they didn't mend their ways.

However, the stories of how Shasm-Zha and Posai celebrated their victory were only whispered about in certain circles.

Annoyed the Emperor's Admiral had committed suicide on realising his defeat, Shasm-Zha gathered the remaining Admirals on the bridge of the Potentates Galaxy-Class Carrier. Each was given the opportunity to satisfy her lust or lose their head. The terrified Brittanian failed to achieve any rigidity, even when Posai bent him over and thrust himself into the Admiral's arse. Shasm-Zha laughed as she removed the man's head with a single stroke of her blade.

The Batavian made a valiant effort and attempted cunnilingus. Shasm-Zha sat in the command chair, thighs wrapped around his ginger head as his tongue prodded and probed. Her fingers tangled in his hair, she thrust herself against his face but, in his distress, he never found his timing. He knew he'd failed even before Posai yanked his head back. The knife slashed and Shasm-Zha shuddered with the pleasure of being showered in warm blood.

Unable to contain himself, Posai pulled Shasm-Zha into the congealing pool. They fucked without constraint, biting, scratching and tearing at each other as they swam in the naval blood. The third Admiral watched on.

The Arberian was a dark-haired woman with brilliant blue eyes. It was rumoured she was the favoured plaything of mad Queen Maria XI. If she felt her gender gave her any advantage over her now headless colleagues, she was wrong. Whilst being fucked by Posai from behind, Shasm-Zha eyed up the remaining Admiral like a predator. She beckoned for the woman to join her. The Arberian latched on to the pirate's nipples. She wasn't gentle – pinching and leaving bite marks. Shasm-Zha screeched with pleasure but did not orgasm.

Posai withdrew from his wife, and she slid over the Arberian Admiral until mouths met cunts. The Admiral slipped two, then three, fingers into the pirate's cunt, moving with deliberate rhythm. Posai stood over the writhing bodies, working his cock. He came first, his semen turning pink as it mixed with the blood smeared over his wife's back.

Shasm-Zha's tongue lashed. The Admiral lost herself. In submitting to her own pleasure, she failed to finish off her conqueror and lost her head. Shasm-Zha yelled in triumph when her husband's mouth managed what the Admiral's couldn't.

• • • •

While the Red Banner Fleet cheered the broadcast, the Potentates watched in horror. None more so than the Emperor, who realised he'd lost twice over and was about to get royally fucked.

Mad Queen Maria was infuriated by the demise of her favoured plaything and the destruction of her naval fleet. The Emperor prostrated himself – it wasn't enough. True to their wager, the mad Queen strapped on an enormous dildo, bent him over a chair and proceeded to fuck him. At the same time, he was forced to swallow the fat cock of the Grand Pensionary Pieter van de Spiegel, who grasped him firmly by the ears as he thrust in time with the mad Queen.

Once they'd finished with him, they joined the Empress in a cold beverage by the window. Thinking his humiliation was over, the Emperor stood up, but was forced back onto all fours by Queen Matilda, who thrashed his naked arse with a leather strap. As a final indignity, he was ridden like a horse by a naked King Stephen and, every time he slowed, Queen Matilda whipped him again. He'd very much misunderstood their reference to horseplay when taking their wager.

The Empress took control of matters, offering gifts to her most esteemed trading partners in a gesture of conciliation. To the mad Queen Maria XI, the Empress gifted her husband. She later heard it had taken many months, and the benefaction of most of the Queen's court, before the new plaything had submitted to its role.

To King Stephen and Queen Matilda, she gifted the Emperor's only son, the issue of one of his many concubines. He was a simple but sturdy young man, well built for the rigours of royal horseplay.

As for the Grand Pensionary Pieter van de Spiegel, impressed by the girth of the cock he'd forced down her husband's throat, the Empress invited him to her private chambers to negotiate his recompense. She welcomed him on her knees, her rose-painted lips parted in welcome. Unbeknownst to the general population, the Empress had also spent her younger days as a Flower Girl. Her negotiations with the Grand Pensionary of the Batavian Cluster continued on and off for well over a decade.

· · · ·

After the defeat of the Potentatial Naval Fleet, regular pirating held no further interest for Shasm-Zha. She had no desire to be hunted for the rest of her life. With the most trustworthy leader of her farmer planets as intermediary, she arranged a meeting with the Empress to negotiate her retirement.

By mutual agreement, their secret rendezvous was held on one of the Flower Ships. A great deal of money was paid to ensure no other clients were anywhere near the ships. As a further disguise, each woman dressed in a traditional, figure-hugging gown, and wore thick make-up and lacquered hair.

The two former-Flower Girls dipped their heads and dropped to their knees in greeting, then settled onto cushions side-by-side. Whilst the two most powerful women in the Empire whispered behind fluttering fans, Flower Girls served them drinks. When two young girls began to sing, the Empress waved them from the room.

Alone, the women folded their fans and turned to face each other. The Empress slid a finger between the pirate's legendary, red-stained lips. Shasm-Zha, holding the Empress' gaze as well as her hands, sucked and flicked her tongue until she'd tasted all ten digits.

Discussion of the economic benefits of retirement commenced with the undoing of gowns, the silk sliding off their shoulders into piles of pink and red. The Empress ran her fingernail down Shasm-Zha's bicep, leaving a red mark. Shasm-Zha pulled the Empress forward by the nipples till their lips collided.

They took great care not to disturb their lacquered hair as they negotiated each other's bodies. Shasm-Zha parried with her tongue and fingers in defense of her political, legal and economic position. The Empress' second orgasm won the pirate the right to keep all the profits from her years of piracy. With Shasm-Zha's nipple between her teeth, the Empress won back her pillaged Imperial Navy vessels, complete with their upgraded bio-mechanical propulsion complexes.

On the edge of her third orgasm, the Empress agreed Shasm-Zha should retire to the Capital Planet of the Empire. Her legs spread to accommodate the Empress' hair arrangement between her thighs, Shasm-Zha cried out her consent for Posai to advise the Empress in matters of economics and military strategy.

Later, as they rocked cunt-to-cunt, arms and legs tangled together, the Empress and the soon-to-be-retired Pirate agreed it would be beneficial to meet in this way on a regular basis.

• • • •

And so, the most fearsome pirate to roam the known universe, retired from her conquest of the stars. With the Empress' endorsement, she established a string of planet-based luxury brothels to entertain the stream of dignitaries who visited for trade negotiations.

Shasm-Zha and Posai were often called to the Palace to assist the Empress in her parlays with the Grand Pensionary of the Batavian Cluster. Their assistance didn't seem to help advance the negotiations at all.

TOO LATE FOR SORRY

You can say you're sorry as many times as you like, but it will make no difference. I'll never forgive you. I can't believe you didn't warn me. You just let me wander in blind, with no idea of who she was and how she lied.

You were truthful when you spoke of her beauty, even though you failed to describe her pale lips and clear green eyes. But you gave me no hint of her violence and her love of inflicting pain. By the time I realised, it was too late.

She never seemed real and maybe she never was? Have you tried to find her? I have. She's never where I look and her absence cuts deep. I miss the darkness of her hair and the mad gleam in her eye. But, most of all I miss her cruelty, the way she made me hurt.

You keep saying you're sorry, but I just don't believe you. I think you know where she is. I think you know who she is. I think you know what she is. What I think you don't know, is who I am.

So, you can just hang here a little longer. The cuts I've made may be small, but they are many. And, while your life-blood drips away, it's not pain you feel, it's regret. She taught me this – how to make you responsible for your own pain.

All you had to do was warn me.

TRADER OF FANTASIES

Ramiel did as he had been instructed and entered the wooden shack without knocking. Before him stood a woman, her entire body wreathed in flames. Her red hair was tucked behind elven ears and hung almost to the floor. She stared at him with deep amber eyes then smiled, full lips parting to reveal gleaming long canines. She was the most beautiful creature he'd ever seen.

It was several moments before he noticed the room. The floor was covered with furs and enormous soft cushions were scattered around the fireplace. On one of the cushions a gigantic purring lynx was curled up in a tight ball. The only furniture in the room was a small table, upon which sat a tray of glasses and a bottle of whiskey.

Three of the room's four walls were hung with rich tapestries of gold, red, cream and green, each depicting naked figures in varying states of sexual ecstasy. But it was the fourth wall Ramiel had come for. It was lined with books, thousands of them, all bound in soft leathers of red, cream and green. He fell to his knees at the sight of them, overwhelmed by the magnificent, decadent, illegality of what was before him.

These were her fabled treasure, her secret, and her weapon. Books hidden from the authorities. Not books of revolution or rebellion – not these books. These books contained dreams and hopes. The fantasies found on the fine, crisp gold embossed pages were erotic, subversive and challenging to the nature of the city and its rulers. They were at once delicious and dangerous.

"Welcome. I am Iculisma." Her voice was deep. "You have the payment?"

Ramiel held out his hand to reveal the two silver coins. She pointed to a small black lacquered box to his left. He lifted the lid and dropped the coins inside, where they joined many others.

43

"Before I decide if you may read, I have three questions. I advise you to answer fully and honestly if you wish to partake of my collection. Are you ready?"

Ramiel nodded.

"Who are you?"

"My name is..." his voice scratched in a higher octave than usual, he cleared his throat and started again. "My name is Ramiel; I'm the hangman." He clapped his hand over his mouth, he hadn't meant to say that. No one was meant to know his vocation.

Iculisma nodded, her face impassive. "Why are you here?"

Again, Ramiel was shocked at his answer. "I see death all day, every day. I'm a dispenser of pain and misery, a killer of men and women. I hate what I do and what I've become." Ramiel was terrified. He glanced over his shoulder at the door just behind him, wondering if it was too late to make a run for it.

"What are you seeking?"

Once more his words emerged unbidden, "I want someone to pamper, someone to give pleasure to. I want to make someone happy and fulfilled. I want to be the joy in someone's life."

"You want sex?" she prompted.

"Yes. No. Yes, I want sex, but not just sex..." He paused; his brow furrowed as he thought. "I want more. I want someone to love." He shrugged and hung his head, waiting for her to laugh and send him away.

"Look at me," she instructed. The fire around her form faded away and a woman stood before him, now sheathed in a translucent and sparkling moss-coloured dress. This time, her smile warmed right through to her remarkable eyes. "I'm so pleased you found me Ramiel. Come and sit by the fire while I search for your book."

Ramiel's eyes filled with tears, and he let out a half sob. He stumbled forward to a large deep red cushion, suitably far away from the enormous cat.

"Whiskey?" Iculisma enquired.

"Yes, please." Ramiel's reply was again unexpected. He didn't drink, it wasn't safe to lose control in his profession.

Her hand brushed his as she passed him his drink. The heat of her touch burst through his body, exciting and stirring him in ways he'd never experienced. Hand shaking, he sipped the whiskey, hoping the smoky amber liquid would settle his nerves.

Iculisma moved to the wall of books. Her hand stroked their spines, one after another. After several minutes, she selected a small volume with a red cover. She held the book in her hand, weighing it for a moment, before nodding and returning to the fire. She sank into the cushion next to him, glass of whiskey in one hand, book in the other.

"This is your story, Ramiel. You can read it yourself or, if you prefer, I can read it to you."

"I ... I can read it myself, thank you," he said.

Her hot fingers again grazed his as she placed the book in his palm. He lifted the book to his nose, inhaled its aroma, and sighed with pleasure. Then he opened the front cover and started to read.

The hero, a lonely figure, is surrounded by violence and devoid of affection. He happens upon a wretched young man, Emile, who has been forced onto the streets. Trading sex for survival, Emile has been beaten by his last customer. Desperate, he keeps working despite his injuries. The hero takes the man home to his rooms, where he bathes him and tends his wounds.

Ramiel nodded with understanding at the hero's misery and almost wept at the descriptions of Emile's injuries. Pausing only to sip on his whiskey, Ramiel sank deeper into the cushion before being swept back into the tale.

Emile is suspicious of the hero's motives, thinking he wants to own him and sell him for his own profit. He's torn between his distrust of people and a growing affection for the hero. He offers himself to the hero and is confused and angry when he's refused.

Ramiel was bewildered when the hero rejected the offer. The detailed and vivid description of Emile's naked advances had aroused him, or perhaps it was his proximity to Iculisma, her translucent dress and the muskiness of her perfume? He wiped beads of sweat from his top lip and once again lost himself in the story.

Thinking the hero finds him disgusting, Emile leaves and returns to the violence and degradation of the streets. The hero mourns his departure. His own life of violence and death has not equipped him for love.

Tears trailed down Ramiel's cheeks.

The hero searches the streets until, at the point of giving up, he finds Emile in a dark alley he'd almost missed. Standing over him is the customer who beat him before, this time he is murderous. Just in time the hero steps in. The customer, recognising him, runs away in fear. Sweeping Emile into his arms, the hero strides back to his rooms. He expresses his love in ways Emile had never imagined possible. Emile repays those affections with his own. No words of love are required.

No longer sure if he was the reader or the hero, Ramiel closed the book and placed it in Iculisma's outstretched hand. He drained the glass of whiskey.

Iculisma's smile was soft and tender. "Was that the story you wished to read?"

Incapable of talking, Ramiel nodded.

"I am so pleased." Iculisma stood and stretched. "You're welcome to another whiskey before you leave. Maybe next time you come to see me, you'll bring a friend?"

Before Ramiel had a chance to reply that he had no friends, Iculisma had disappeared behind one of the tapestries, leaving him alone with the lynx. No longer purring, the cat regarded him with large green eyes, tufted ears alert and short tail flicking. After a final gaze at the wall of books, Ramiel gathered himself together and let himself out.

Without knowing why, he felt compelled to take a different route home.

• • • •

Danger and death hung in the air of the dark alley like old friends. Antos stood over a cowering figure. He had yet to act on his urge to murder his victims. This one, he decided, would be his first.

Antos drew his weapon as a man strode toward him. Then his eyes widened in terror. Behind the stranger stood a towering woman wrapped in flames, her flaming hair threw sparks as it snaked and shimmered around her head. He could feel her fire inside his head and when she shrieked his name, Antos turned and fled.

Blind and deaf to the spectre behind him, Ramiel knelt and brushed aside the hair draped across the cowering victim's face.

"Emile!" he gasped in surprise.

Emile stared back at him, "Ramiel?"

• • • •

Iculisma slipped out of the alley and left her two clients to their destiny. The lynx would take care of Antos. On her way back to her shack, she stopped at the Kraken Arms for a well-deserved whiskey. After all, it wasn't every day she managed to weave two stories together so well.

YOU ARE ALREADY DEAD

Of my family I have very little recollection. I was taken from them and they from me. My memories have become unreliable facsimiles of their truth, distorted by pain. Even the world upon which they existed has been reduced to cosmic dust.

Of myself, however, there is so much to say I struggle to know where to begin.

My abduction seems the obvious starting point and yet it is not. In truth the start lies in a cluster of random mutations in my genetic code. A simple transposition here and a mismatch of base pairs there. The sum of which resulted in me being a little less human than the rest. Or perhaps a little more human? Whichever is of no importance. What matters is at puberty, when those altered genes expressed themselves, I set off every alarm in the galaxy – and a few beyond that.

I was identified as a monster, a living weapon.

You came for me from every direction and enormous distance. If I had known my abilities then, I could have saved my people and my world but, too young and unaware of my talents, I did nothing.

In the war that erupted, everyone and everything I had known to exist was destroyed. I have carried that guilt ever since, along with the desire for revenge.

As in all war, to the victor go the spoils. I – a lost and angry child – was the spoils and to the victor I went. Despite being taken against my will, if they had shown love and affection, or even a little empathy, I would have embraced them and rewarded them with devotion. These soft emotions were not part of their way of life and instead they feared what I would do with my trauma. The fearful do terrible things.

I was held immobile in absolute darkness and silence. Entombed. It is a most terrifying thing to be disconnected from all sensation against one's will. Even touch loses its meaning without any of the other senses to guide it.

In the absence of external stimuli, the mind expands, desperate to fill the sensory gaps. Chemical reactions crackle as the nervous system invents physical input to replace the nothing it receives. False images dance in front of unseeing eyes. Heart-pumped blood becomes a raging river – valves thud shut then swish open to manage the wild torrent. To breathe is to unleash a cyclone – the winds howl in, there is silence in the eye of the storm, then the winds scream out.

In that dark, silent tomb a never-ending tempest raged within me. I taught myself to embrace the storm and shed the too brief learnings of who I had been. As my humanity diminished, I became what they feared. Their tomb had become my womb and it birthed a being for whom the laws of the universe hold no meaning.

I became their monster, a living weapon.

My captors had waged a war against all others to possess me. If they wanted to use what they had fought for, they were forced to provide for me. They could not keep me both entombed and alive. Even a monster requires the necessities of life.

The first time they opened my tomb I did almost nothing but observe. They had afforded their ship the double protection of further containing me within a dampened cell. Despite the low light and muted sound, it took me a moment to orient myself as my senses adjusted to the flood of stimuli. I was joined by two guards.

They were tall and, even with the encumbrance of their protective suits, slender. Behind the visors of their helmets, red eyes glowed in reptilian visages. The sight of them had terrified the human-child who had been me. To monster-me, they looked frail, temporary and inconsequential. It amused me they felt safe in their suits.

They fed me and provided for my ablutions. I will not deny that part of me was tempted to throw my bodily wastes at the guards, but such an act would have just been petty. Monsters don't waste their time on pettiness – monsters look for weaknesses to exploit. So, I studied them, with all my starved senses.

The shorter of the two had a tic. Every time I looked at her, she tapped the two fingers of her right hand against her hip – as if reaching for an absent weapon. I was tempted to test whether I could stop the tapping, but revenge requires patience, and I wanted them complacent.

The other guard was better at hiding her emotions, but her heart rate and respiration jumped each time I moved. I recognised that storm. She was just as terrified as her companion. Despite my best intentions I smiled, baring as many of my teeth as possible. They both took a step backwards at my aggressive act.

I laughed. The sound was like nails on a chalkboard – discordant and aggressive. The shorter guard's finger tapping became a grabbing motion, and the combined sound of their hearts pounding and rasping breaths was almost deafening. I stepped back into my tomb to ponder my new-found knowledge in peace. The dark silence and absence of sensation a welcome respite.

Time no longer had meaning. Between openings of my tomb, I could have a sole heartbeat or millions, I could contemplate a single idea or devise an entire mathematical theory along with mental proofs. My mind had become extraordinary and like any weapon needed rigorous testing. During my release times I continued to experiment on my subjects and observed their responses.

It wasn't long before I could control every aspect of the ship's crew from their digestive system to their thoughts. If I had wished I could have killed them on the spot in any number of ways, but there would have been no joy for me in that. Revenge requires inflicting maximum suffering and an acknowledgment of being bested. Every monster knows this. Revenge is never humane.

Today, I emerge from my tomb to discover new surroundings. I have been transplanted, taken from their ship and embedded into a space station. To accentuate the shift, the crew have also changed. I miss my guard with her finger-tapping tic, but she has served her purpose and the new guards believe me to be submissive and compliant. They still wear their helmets when they enter the buffered cell, in the belief they are protected. They underestimate what I am.

I know all I need within moments of my emergence.

The station circles their home planet in a low geosynchronous orbit. It is tethered to an equatorial mountain by a tectonic powered space elevator. To counteract gravity and hold the station in position, the tether extends well beyond the station into space. Like an umbilical cord the elevator delivers all the station's needs and removes its waste. It also gives me access to so much more than their minds.

I abandon the buffered cell and the protection of my tomb to stroll the station. My movements, though casual, are not aimless. I am heading to the station's control room. My captors destroyed my world, and today, I will return the favour. Unbeknownst to them, I control not only their every act and thought, but their entire planet.

I control yours too, for even though they were the victors, you would have been no different. Had you not warred with them to possess me, then my planet, country and family would have survived. Do not forget I seek only revenge, revenge on all, and I already have it.

For, I am a monster, a living weapon.

You are already dead, but I leave you just enough of your perceived time to contemplate what you have brought upon yourselves.

I told you I was beyond the laws of the universe – time, space, and the conservation of energy mean nothing to me. The core of this planet, and of every world who came for me, is heating at an exponential rate. To make myself clear, almost every inhabited planet in the galaxy is melting. You will soon be swimming in magma, reduced to your component elements.

As for myself, I have severed the tether beyond the station. Every alarm is sounding – klaxons, whistles and bells mix with shouts and screams as the station's crew realise what I have done. This act of sabotage will cost me my life, but I have won.

We are falling.

In the control room, the station commander stands resolute before me – the only member of the crew not consumed by their collective panic. She stares at me with her unblinking red eyes. I hope she sees the monster, the living weapon they created, for what I truly am – an all-powerful lost, angry and insane child with nothing to lose.

I smile. With a nod of defeat, she sits, folds her long legs in the strange way of her kind and makes her final station-wide announcement.

"Going down!"

SECRETS

We visited the witch together. Hitched our skirts to cross gurgling streams and held hands as we approached her stone cottage deep in the lush green forest. We gave her our life's savings and handed her the scribbled lists of requirements for our true loves.

After reading our desires, the witch stared at us with sad eyes. She offered us each a tisane, brewed from gathered herbs and flowers. We were sure the bitter elixir was a love potion. She whispered first into your ear, and then into mine. We left. Each with our secret locked deep inside where forbidden knowledge resides.

Days, weeks, months and years passed. Our knights in shining armour never came knocking on our door.

Instead of marrying we worked our fields together all the days long. We baked bread, made blackberry jam and embraced our spinsterhood.

On nights illuminated by the full moon we danced. Hand-in-hand we swayed to music only we could hear; our secrets simmering close to the surface. The villagers found us this way one late summer eve.

We didn't scream as we burned. The only sounds that passed our melting lips were secrets – too long held. We spoke each other's name. In death came clarity. All those years ago the witch had seen our truth, but in life we'd been too afraid to accept it.

Released from the inhibitions of the living we haunt our murderers with moans of ecstasy. Our wraith-like figures drift through walls entwined in passion.

On nights illuminated by the full moon we invite the young village women to join us in our naked dance. We sway to our own music. There are no more secrets.

THE ABYSS

The first time your feet touch the briny waters of the ocean, you feel the inky black of an abyss other than your own. You hitch your skirt up above your knees and bury your delicate pink toes into the soft sand. This is the day you feel her song – your blood pumps in time with the melody. The water swirls around your ankles and licks up your calves. The waves, like your eyes, a foamy green. With every surge of the tide, you feel her tug, pulling you seaward.

Ever since your childhood was taken at the hand of a devil disguised as God, you've maintained an image of sombre restraint. Today you change. A violent gust of wind tears your hair free from its pins. Your habitual frown turns into a smile. For the first time you feel happy. Her song, thrumming in your veins, fills you with joy. This is the day your black heart is touched by a kindred spirit.

Abandoning her call is difficult, but you resist. Despite your resolve to leave, you tarry too long, travel home in wet clothes and are overwhelmed by a fever before dawn. In your delirium, you sing vile shanties known only to pirates and naval conscripts – your parents are appalled. When they plunge you into an ice-cold bath to cool the fever, your songs get worse. The Pastor is called before nightfall.

He prays at your bedside for hours. All the while you sway in time with the tide and sing of rum and whores. Sometime in the midnight hours, the abyss wells up and douses the fever. Inky clouds of black flood your sea-green eyes.

You fling back the bedcovers and tear off your nightgown. Thanking his God, the Pastor embraces you, as he has done so often since you were but a girl. You are no longer that submissive child.

Long after you have left, his cold, ruined body will be discovered – sea foam spilling from his blue lips.

The full moon shines a path along the waterway that borders your family's farm. Silvery fish dart under rocks and hide amongst the willow roots as you splash your way towards the coast. The taste of the sea draws dark-skinned eels from the shadows as you pass. Unable to resist the call of their first home, a writhing mass of them follow you on your journey.

The drain becomes a creek, becomes a stream, becomes a river, which empties into a harbour. Washed clean, you float amongst the flotsam. Swept along by the tide, you sing along with her, the song now primal, it uses no words but calls to blood. A fisherman shouts from the pier and dives in to save you. Like the Pastor, he succumbs to your embrace – you leave his body to the eels.

The current sucks you beyond the town, through the channel, beyond the shore, and out towards the horizon. Onwards you float, gripped by a torrent you couldn't escape even if you wished to.

Gathering clouds catch the morning sun's first rays, turning the sky pink then a vivid blood-orange – the colours pain your eyes. Waves rise in sharp peaks and wind-tossed spume fills the air. You sink beneath the surface. At first, you hold your breath in fear then, accepting your fate, you inhale. Instead of the anticipated pain, a cool calm suffuses your body. You're home.

The changes that began on the beach now come to completion. Delicate pink fins trail down your limbs and fringe elongated fingers and toes. Millions of fine silver scales emerge from your skin, they shimmer as you swim. When you smile, the gash that was your mouth widens, and your tongue flicks across rows of serrated teeth. You have been transmogrified – no longer a creature of the land, now a denizen of the deep.

You sink deeper, leaving the storm at the surface behind, drawn into the calm by her song and the chorus of your sisters. So many of you. All born of pain. Called away from the despair of the light and into the black depths of the abyss.

She entwines you in her tentacles and pulls you close. The kraken's love is absolute – your devotion is total.

You embrace your sisters and share your songs of betrayal and abuse with them. They sing theirs in return. Your tears become the ocean, and your pain feeds the storm. Prey become predator – you're ready for the hunt.

You rise to the surface to claim your revenge. You and your sisters ride the crests of giant waves singing your victims to their doom. The guilty fling themselves into your deadly embrace – sails are left flapping and ships to flounder. Screams fill the air. Tentacles rise from the abyss. Hulls are torn apart and masts crack like twigs.

Years, decades, and centuries pass. The ships change – their engines pound without stop, and the ocean is filled with the noise. Your songs are unable to penetrate the cacophony. Crews no longer fill the decks and dive to save you, they hide away within their steel shells distracted by technologies beyond your ken.

What never ceases is the flow of new sisters joining you in the abyss. Abuse continues to spawn new sea-devils, all drawn to the depths by the song of the kraken. Transformed from victims, they too are ravenous for revenge. Their fresh fury feeds your own.

Despite the changes of time, deep in the abyss, the kraken still sings her song. As always, you join her – your hunger never sated. On nights when the moon is full and the sea is calm, you and your sisters swarm to the surface, your voices joined in song.

Under the pressure of her tentacles, even steel cracks. Above the sound of rending metal, men scream – until they hear your song. Enthralled, they flounder towards you, all sense replaced by an aching need. They are few and you are many, only the minutest of scraps escape to be swept up by plankton.

Far from satisfied, you and your sisters return to the inky depths of the abyss. Tangled in the tentacled embrace of the kraken you wait. All the while you sing.

PERSUASION

Even with her back to the door there's enough light from the small grimy side window for me to appreciate the new arrival. She's dressed entirely in black. Tight leather pants hug curvaceous thighs and sturdy calves, their muscularity accentuated by the height of the diamante stilettos she wears. Pale breasts threaten to spill over the top of her satin bustier.

She stares around the bar as if searching for someone specific, her golden eyes flicking from face to face until they come to me. She pauses and tilts her head. Flaming waves of hair cascade to one side exposing an upstanding pointed ear. I'm no elf expert but given her colouration and curves, I'm pretty sure she's a Fire-Elf. To dispel any doubt a small flame flickers around her fingertips. A murmur sweeps around the room and a couple of dwarves stand and leave without finishing their drinks. Not everyone can handle a Fire-Elf.

With a nod to the goblin behind the bar, she saunters in my direction. The goblin's hand shakes as he pours a generous measure of fire-spirit. The glass appears on my table without his aid. I grab my glass of wine and wish it contained something a little stronger.

She leans forward until her face hovers just before mine. I resist the urge to reach out to prevent her magnificent breasts tumbling forth, by some magic they stay restrained.

"You need company."

It wasn't a question. She slides onto the bench seat of the cubicle beside me. It's awkward for me to shuffle over. My wings won't behave. I'm certain they're why she's chosen me. She leans in and with the merest of touches traces a fingertip across their soft gossamer. I do my best to tuck them behind me but, the traitorous appendages they are, they quiver with delight and flutter closer to her touch.

"What's your name?" Her voice is deep and husky.

"Perpetua."

"Perpetua...Perpetua...Per...pet...ua," she plays with my name. "Pretty Perpetua, are you open to persuasion?"

"Perhaps." I'm aghast at the alliteration but my wings are radiating sparks of pleasure and I can't think clearly.

I think you are, my pretty Perpetua. We're going to have such fun.

Oh, by the flowers of the forest...she's inside my head.

My wings are beating so hard they've lifted me out of the cubicle and I'm hovering beside her. She stands and slips her hand into mine. I think it's to hold me in place but then the room blurs and we're outside. Not just outside but somewhere else altogether. She's powerful this Fire Elf, she's found my dream location. I let her pull me into her arms.

My fingers drift across her satiny mounds. It only takes a gentle flick of my thumb for them to burst out, in freedom they are full and round. Her nipples, the palest of pink, scrunch tight in the cool air of the forest. She chuckles from the back of her throat when I pinch them.

Somehow, she's managed to slip my halter-neck dress off, the cloud of purple spider silk wafts to the forest floor. I'm exposed. Her golden eyes glitter with flashes of red. She runs her gaze over my small breasts, down past my waist and across the soft curve of my belly. The glitter turns to a blaze as her eyes come to rest on my mons Venus. It's already glowing, pulsing with a silvery-blue shimmer to match the lights flashing across my wings. It is obvious I need no persuasion.

Her mouth is hot and her tongue tastes of whiskey. She's firm but not rough. I pinch her nipples again and her heat flares. Grasping the short spikes of my pale green hair she pulls my head back to expose my neck. Her tongue slides from my ear, down my neck then lower. Lips wrap around my nipple. Flashes of red streak across my wings.

I flutter higher. Her mouth and tongue trail down my body, until I wrap my legs around her neck. Her tongue plunges inside my glowing cunt with a heat I've never experienced. It's almost too hot to endure.

Almost.

My insides turn molten and I melt into her palm. The birds are silenced by my screams of delight. Sated and gasping for breath, I flutter to the forest floor. My knees sink into soft moss.

With her help, I peel her out of her pants, one leg at a time. My wings flutter across her nipples, the hard edges beating so fast they're a blur. She groans. I slide cool fingers up her inner thighs and penetrate the flaming thicket surrounding her hot cunt. I plunge deep. She arches against my fingers, but I know what she really wants.

Still standing, she opens her legs at my nudge, and I crawl underneath. My glowing red wings beat against her, all four of them pound her in rapid succession. I can't see her face but, from her moans, I know she's about to come. My body joins hers in mutual orgasm.

She cries out in ecstasy. I shriek my words of magic.

Silly Fire-Elf. She asked my name, but she should have asked who I am.

I'm a Fancier-Fairy. I specialise in finding, collecting, and appreciating gorgeous, sexy things. And she's mine now. Mine to keep forever.

The miniature Fire-Elf flaming in fury in a palm-sized glass bell really is the jewel in my collection. She's unique in the known world and my fellow Fancier-Fairies come from far and wide to admire her.

I call her Persuasion.

TEA

I realise there's more in my cup than tea when the crumbs from my biscuit begin to tumble down my front in a cascade that splashes and pools in the folds of my skirt. Before me, the Chinese woman I'm consulting settles her cup back on its saucer. On her lap, the dog's eyes grow large, and galaxies whirl within their blackness.

The room flexes, the walls moving in time with my breathing. Through the window, I see the garden. Flowers, full of the hopes of spring, dissolve into a Monet-like canvas, savaged by a suicidal Van Gogh. To each side of the masterpiece, red curtains flow hot and liquid to the floor. Steam rises where they spill across ice-cold floorboards.

Lost in the beauty of the illusion, I forget what brought me here. The relief is sweet. I feel euphoric, weightless, free. Like before. Like the very first time she held my face and kissed me, her lips soft and tongue sure. She tasted of strawberries. Before. Before I did what I did.

"You came about your demons?" The dog speaks.

"Yes, where are they?"

"You know where they are. You have to look deep within yourself to find them."

I know the dog speaks only truth – galaxies don't lie. But I fear myself and what I'll find if I look. I'm unprotected and exposed.

The Chinese woman pours more tea. The spout forced between my lips, the bitter liquid fills my mouth and slides down my throat. Words poised to argue drown in the amber flood.

I see beyond the barriers I've constructed. Fresh-sprouted wings lift me to the ceiling, from where I see the events play out like a film. Frames flicker between colour and black and white as they skip and skitter through time. The past and the present together, happening at once.

She's here and she's not. I love her and I despise her. She's alive and...I'm innocent and I'm guilty and innocent and guilty and I'm guilty and I'm alone with her. And I'm alone. My wings falter. They rip and shred.

Brittle, I fall and shatter on impact. Jagged shards of me jut out at rude angles. A purple gash of melancholy, a crimson streak of rage, a bolt of jaundiced cowardice – all enveloped in the reality-altering black of my guilt.

The room fills with absence. All that remains is a jewel-like galaxy. It glitters at the fringe of the blackness, within it sits a Chinese woman and a dog who speaks for her. The voice ripples across the void to reach me.

"I see much now, but your demons are well hidden. Try harder."

I wade through a pool of iridescent memories, watching them splash and churn in my wake. The ones I seek slither around my ankles, twisting and pulling me into the darkest depths of my own abyss. They flow into my every orifice. I'm drowning.

Her tongue, which has brought me such ecstasy, shapes words to cut – I slash back. The blackness melts in the heat of my rage. Life-blood spurts in a never-ending hot stream. Its metallic aroma pungent and rich. The perfume of death.

For this, my demons emerge.

The room shifts and shudders. A table set with tea and biscuits slides into view and settles in front of me. I sit in a high-backed chair, still holding a cup and saucer. The rough texture of the matte glaze grazes the tips of my fingers. The lapdog has moved to a cushion in the bay window. It's curled in a tight ball of sleep, emitting the soft snorts typical of its breed. Sanguine chiffon drapes sway in the cooling air of the late afternoon.

The Chinese woman remains seated across from me – her expression tells me nothing. She takes a sip of tea, smacks her lips and with deliberate care places the delicate cup and saucer on the table. I place mine alongside the matching teapot.

"It is fortunate that you have come to me. I have seen and felt your demons. They are some of the cruellest and violent I have ever encountered, but they are not beyond my skills."

From within the folds of her loose jacket she draws out a jade box and places it on the table. Carved into the delicate beauty of the translucent green stone are images of the foulest of oriental demons. She lifts the lid to reveal the tools of her trade. Jade acupuncture needles.

"These needles have been used to banish demons for over a thousand years." She picks one up to show me how fine and perfect they are. "Now I understand the nature of your demons I know how and where to place the needles to banish them."

The Chinese woman stands, "We must not lose any more time." She beckons for me to follow.

I push myself up out of the chair. I'm surprised by the shower of crumbs that fall from the folds in my skirt and scatter across the floor around my feet.

She flaps her hand. "Of no consequence, come."

Unable to delay any longer, I clear my throat to gain her attention.

"Madam, I thank you for your efforts, but I'm afraid you've misunderstood my intentions. I didn't come to you to have my demons exorcised – I came to find them."

Without waiting for her response, I pull an envelope thick with cash from the pocket of my skirt and place it on the table next to the red and black tea set. I help myself to another biscuit and walk from the room.

The demons remain with me when I leave, their terrible presence a comfort.

Knowing the torment to come, I feel only relief.

.

THE POET, THE MANUCHURIAN, AND I

As we sail from Kefalonia I read the poet's words aloud. At first my lips and tongue struggle to find the rhythm – the meter stilted and stiff. My fingers drum the beat. The words begin to flow and expand beyond their meanings to become emotions. I recite them with a tremor in my voice. They are old but reach across time to speak to me.

The poet's words creep under my skin and writhe their way into my hardened heart. He speaks of things that have meaning to me: the journey; the riches; the knowledge.

He speaks of Ithaka.

We sail on a calm sea towards her shores. As the poet instructs, a rare excitement fills both my spirit and body. I don't understand what I'm seeking, but I'm poised and ready to find my reward.

The poet urges me to stop and buy fine things at Phoenician trading stations. How I'd love to purchase their ampules of sensual perfumes and drape their lengths of brilliant cloth around my body. If only the Phoenicians still traded, I would twist strings of glass beads around my neck and sample wine from their terracotta jars.

I arrive in Ithaka rich with all I have learned in my long travels. Knowledge gleaned not from the teachings of Egyptian scholars, but from the journey itself. My journey to Ithaka has been long, stretching into years.

Not every harbour I visited along the way filled me with happiness. On my journey within, naked and undefended by champions, I faced the angry Poseidon and his monstrous companions. Against the poet's advice, I carry the monsters with me as trophies of my strength. I'm never alone.

The poet concludes Ithaka has nothing more to give me. To him, the voyage has been the prize. In that, he could not be more wrong.

My crew and I sail into this new harbour. The men gather, and quarrel, helping with lines and moorings. My heart fills with joy and delight at the attention and affection directed our way. I respond. Smiling, flirting and teasing in turn. The salt-laden air fills with expectation and possibility, lifting me into an exalted state of wildness.

Well met by locals and visitors alike, wine and spirits flow in every taverna. New friends drawn to my joy and playfulness embrace me as though we've been life-time acquaintances.

The Manchurian is here. He's not at all what I expected. Loud and arrogant, tall, and proud in his youth. Our eyes meet. He draws me in, demanding my lips. I give him what he commands without seriousness, laugh at his surprise, and return to my crew. We continue on our way, howling under the moon as we trail the laneways of the port.

Our cabins beckon as we approach our ship. The day has been long and full, and the evening longer. I drift past. The lights and sounds of the next taverna lure me in. He's there. His lips twitching into a smile as he points at them. Our kiss lingers, deepens then softens until we withdraw for air.

Wine flows. Voices rise and fall. We are mocked and derided. Our fingers intertwine and we ignore them all. In time, the barbarians, friends, and foe drift away on their own tides.

We're alone.

The Manchurian is seductive and irresistible, but he's not who he seems. He reaches inside me and releases the monsters. It's not the sweet boy who follows me to my cabin. No. It's the Laistrygonian, the Cyclops and the wild Poseidon who accompany me.

The cannibalistic Laistrygonian falls upon me first, consuming my flesh, his lips and teeth grazing at will. I respond, just as savage, using tooth and nail to match his ferocity. We moan and growl as we test our strength against one another. Finding ourselves equally starved, we feast upon each other. My mouth delights in his fresh taste and novel textures. Sated, the Laistrygonian makes way for the Cyclops.

Blind, the giant explores me with practised hands. Firm fingers stroke, probe and dip into my hidden places until no secrets remain between us. I am discovered, exposed and revealed. My cries of joy inflame him to delve deeper and with more precision. Unable to hold myself together, I dissolve in his giant palm.

It's in this state that Poseidon finds me. He gathers me into his arms, muscles flexing as his lips press to mine. The gesture of affection is fleeting. He is no sweet, gentle Olympic God. This is the wild Poseidon of my dreams. He shows no care for my feelings, nor I for his.

Agitated by the passions of their God, the earth rumbles and the oceans surge. There is danger in this union. Perhaps the poet was right? I should not have allowed the monsters into my soul – but how else am I to stir my spirit and body?

I ignore the poet and embrace my lover. Joined, we share a moment of stillness, filled with anticipation and tension. Muscles quiver, then release. Wild Poseidon roars.

Harbour currents roil and the ship strains at its moorings. The sea I carry within my flesh heaves and rises to a crest. I'm drowning in pleasure and the pain of it is excruciating. I ride Poseidon's wave and laugh. There was no danger after all, only release.

The God and I have taken what we desired from each other in Ithaka. He wastes no time on false affection. One final kiss and he's gone. Alone in my shipboard cocoon, I fall into the deep dreamless slumber of the shameless.

Before I rise in the morning the Manchurian has set sail. He leaves only the whisper of his latest conquest on the lips of the few mariners remaining onshore. They sail forth to forget or repeat his words, either way it matters not to me. I have found within myself all the safe anchorage I've ever needed.

Even though my journey has ended, we too set sail. This departure marks the beginning of my voyage back to Ithaka. It may take many years and I may be very old, but we shall meet there again: the poet; the Manchurian; and I.

REDUNDANT

C raig punched the button for the lift. Since the front-page headlines and unflattering television coverage he'd taken to using the grimy service lift from the lower-level car park to his penthouse office. It was a small discomfort but saved him facing the throngs of press in reception and avoided any risk of being accosted by the protesters, who occupied the front steps of the company building.

He'd hoped the unionists would have relented by now, but six weeks into the dispute they still refused to sign the contract. If the bastards wouldn't give in, then more heads would have to roll. As he waited for the lift, Craig flipped through the personnel file for the HR staff. He was sure it was one of those liberal arseholes leaking information to the media, he just needed to figure out which one of them to fire.

The lift doors opened, and he stepped in without bothering to look up. Before he turned to press the button for his floor the lift lurched and began to descend. Confused Craig turned to stare at the control panel. There were no lower floors.

"What the..."

The doors of the lift slid open before Craig had a chance to complete his sentence. In fact, he never had the chance to utter another word ever again.

Before him stood Ramona. Terrifying and magnificent Ramona. The papers in the personnel file fluttered to the floor.

Ramona was a predator, and her preferred prey were men of power. The ugly, abusive and more aggressive the man, the more alluring he was. Craig, being a psychopath, was irresistible. She dragged him into her embrace, wound her swollen abdomen around and plunged her stinger into his arse.

Craig's back arched and shuddered as the venom spread, rendering him paralysed and helpless. Only his eyes were able to express his shock and disbelief.

Ramona carried the still conscious man back to her lair with care. His clothes torn away she inspected him with gentle taps of her antennae. Of special interest his penile projection, it was a little smaller than expected but still swelled to her attentions. Delighted she rubbed his erection until he ejaculated. Her proboscis sucked up the fresh, warm protein-rich semen. On this diet her eggs would grow well.

Craig was still alive two weeks later when, far above him, the Unionists and the Board congratulated each other on signing a revised contract. At the same moment they toasted their missing Company President, Ramona used her antennae to stimulate Craig's flaccid member into life, manipulating him to completion for the last time.

Triggered by the flood of dopamine in Craig's bloodstream the larvae in his belly hatched. Ramona's babies were destructive and relentless. They chewed their way free of his body, stinging and biting each other in fierce competition to emerge and be first to feed on the stream of nutrient-rich semen spread across his belly. What was left of the man when they'd finished was abandoned.

Craig's service was no longer required. He was redundant.

STAR KILLER

I don't know why I return to this little café so often. I can't eat anything they serve, and their version of coffee is terrible. It's not even close to where I'm staying, and of course I can't take my own transport. To get here requires catching two shuttles and a twelve-minute spacewalk.

The first time I stepped out of the airlock was terrifying. The lack of reference to up or down, and the knowledge that a projectile the size of a grain of sand could punch right through my suit, played havoc with my breathing, and sent my adrenalin levels spiking so high my alarm went off. That fear was something new to me, but with time the intensity has mellowed, and the walk is now my favourite part of the trip. Sometimes, I 'go dark' so the illumination from my suit doesn't obscure the millions of spots of starlight, which can be seen from the fringe of this galaxy. It reminds me how very, very small I am, because, in my line of work, I sometimes forget.

No one knows me in the café. If they did, I wouldn't be welcome. Star-killers seldom are. Perhaps this anonymity is part of the appeal. I can drink my dreadful beverage in peace, all the while surrounded by the self-nominated dregs of the universe.

I listen to their conversations, each of them sure they are the worst scum in existence. I chuckle to myself at their hubris. They're mere murderers, thieves, and politicians. I have the taxidermied heads of worse mounted on my walls at home. No one here is worthy of that honour.

Before I became a mass-murderer for hire, collecting heads was a mere hobby. It started with the priest who raped my mother and then forced her to have me. When I was sixteen, he tried to repeat his sins on me. He believed his own lies and convinced himself that being a 'Man of God' made him untouchable.

Despite his perceived divine protection, I touched him–with a knife.

That first attempt at taxidermy was amateurish and clumsy. His eyes bulge, his skin is mottled and most of his hair has fallen out, but it remains my favourite. That first head started me along the career path, which brought me to where I am now.

In the early years, I had no idea I was being observed. My genetic disposition and life circumstances were identified by database trawling bots. Even before I'd stopped wearing nappies my name had been added to a list of potential employees. I've often wondered if the Institute went so far as to cause much of my early trauma to ensure their desired outcome.

By the age of twenty-three I'd become skilled at both murder and taxidermy and my head collection numbered eleven. I lived in a very small country, and my eventual discovery or exposure was inevitable. I'd already been questioned in three of the cases. Before the local authorities could close the net they'd slung around me, I was abducted by the Institute. They also removed my head collection and wiped my existence from all digital records. The odd image or mention of me may still exist in print, but none of it can be corroborated. As far as Aotearoa, and Earth, is concerned, I ceased to exist.

It takes a certain type of personal fortitude to not go insane when faced with being the only human on an interstellar research vessel. I dealt with that and embraced the education and training schedule they set for me. It was a joy to discover my tendencies were celebrated, and even revered. It was the food that caused me to crack. For reasons they've never bothered to explain to me, every second meal they provided me in the first fifty day-cycles was mushrooms on a poor imitation of wholegrain toast. My reaction was unfortunate, it was the second, and last time I killed in anger.

I stayed with the Institute for centuries. It took me that long to pay off my debts and establish my reputation as the best in my field. I also had to buy my own interstellar craft – not just one large enough to live in, but also equipped to securely hold my, now famous, collection of heads. It hadn't taken me long to discover evil was not a trait limited to humanity. Although, not condoned by the Institute, I was never stopped from collecting my trophies.

Being an independent mass-murderer affords me some privileges. One is the ability to scour doomed solar systems for their very worst and keep them as reminders of why I do this job. My collection of heads now numbers in the tens-of-thousands. Once a decade I invite certain colleagues and trainees from the Institute to visit. They come for the food and wine but leave reminded of how personal our craft is. Killing a star is easy if doing so is based in sound reason.

My visits to this café are part of my due diligence. Before I go ahead and destroy a sun, I like to assure myself the native populations of the system are beyond redemption. Even a mass murderer must have a basic code of conduct. My reputation is such that if I refuse a contract, no other Star-killer will take it up. Even my own solar system, despite the ongoing destruction of Earth by humans, survives grace of an intelligent population of tardigrades on a small moon orbiting Jupiter.

I'm disappointed the café hasn't offered up a suitable candidate for my collection of heads. Despite that, I won't be sorry to destroy this solar system when I kill its sun. This café is its only redeeming feature. The sole inhabited planet has been all but destroyed and the native inhabitants unimaginative and ugly. They remind me somehow of mushrooms.

MOTHS TO A FLAME

I hope I'm the last Elf to find herself integrated into an intergalactic spacecraft. I'm not the first of my kind to end up like this. I suspect they intervened with my transition on purpose. Without us Elves the Authorities can't communicate with the Space-Canaries. They need our telepathic skills.

I was still confused when the Authorities ensnared me and failed to fight back. If I could figure out where and when I am I'd be off in a wink, but they're aware of that and keep me moving. They programme my spacecraft to move through the universe in an unpredictable fashion, so I never get a chance to get my bearings.

Three hundred years living in a feudal society means I'm bereft of knowledge of the technology or calculations required to counter their programming. I've applied myself to the educational material they've provided but it's limited in scope to what is useful for my assignments. I now understand the basics of quantum physics but know nothing of multiverse mechanics. So, I'm stuck and have been for the last thirty space years. It's all very frustrating, particularly for an Elf with my particular set of talents.

In an early blow to my confidence, I realised the Authorities were immune to my ability to manipulate minds. On Earth, I influenced the thoughts and actions of others at will. My greatest talent though, is manipulating non-conscious living organisms, especially plants. I induced crops to mature faster and larger than they should, fungi to sprout where they shouldn't and summer fruits to ripen in the middle of winter – all to help those ungrateful humans.

In the early days, those of us born of Old Magic adored those crazy little beasts who called themselves humans. They were so fragile and yet resilient. We couldn't help but protect them from the elements. Before we knew it, they'd overrun the planet and we'd been forced deeper and deeper into the forests, mountain tops and dark hidden places.

By the time I made my decision to leave, there were only pockets of us Elves left in their world. Most had travelled through space and time to the lush green planet of our original universe. For me, the final straw occurred during a particularly harsh winter in France. I'd created a garden of summer vegetables for a starving peasant family. Instead of being grateful they spat at me, called me the devil's whore and trampled the *ungodly* food into the snow.

Here, in the empty space of this particular universe, there are no living entities for me to influence – I can't even create myself a flower to admire. I wish my talents extended to manipulating the elements. If I could influence water I'd fill my pod with it and drown in delight. Some days I imagine I'm one of the mystical Fire Elves. I can almost feel the heat of the burning pod and smell the purple clouds of toxic smoke filling my lungs. Outside of my fantasies, my consciousness doesn't fade away to death. I'm powerless.

Without means to escape, I remain bound within the interior pod of the spacecraft, fed and excavated by tubes. My only company is a Space-Canary and she's as unhappy about the situation as I am. She's tried to communicate her name to me, but it's both incomprehensible and unpronounceable. I call her Rosy.

Given the constraints of my experience, I can only frame my description of Rosy in terms of what I knew on Earth. To my eyes, she resembles an enormous shimmering pink and yellow moth – but less assembled. What might be wings are four times the width of the central portion I refer to as her body. Her head region is a gigantic yellow fluffy ball with two enormous feather-like antennae projecting forwards. She's covered in what appears like a downy fur but is, in fact, a mass of sensory organs. She can't see or hear so feels her way through space by virtue of her extraordinary sense of smell and her ability to sense touch at a molecular level.

Like me, Rosy is hard-wired to the spacecraft, tethered by a flexible harness like a horse to a carriage. Together, we form a functioning unit.

She collects and interprets the data, I translate her findings, and the spacecraft relays it all back to the Authorities. We're an efficient, but miserable, team.

Over the years, Rosy and I have become so close we can sense the subtle nuances in each other's thoughts and in this way, we have our private conversations. The Authorities are privy to all the translations in my head, but they are insensitive to the tone and tenor of the words.

Our purpose is to monitor the smells of space. Rosy has taught me that different sections of space have characteristic odours reflecting the molecular make-up of each region. Deep space smells like hot metal, while the centres of some galaxies have an aroma reminiscent of raspberries. I enjoy her interpretation of those galaxies, but not all assignments are so pleasant. We were once sent to a large galaxy the Authorities believed was becoming unstable. In one of its solar systems was a multi-mooned planet that stank like human flatulence. It took over a light week for Rosy to clean herself, not satisfied until she'd removed every single offending molecule.

From my studies, I know that inappropriate smells in space indicate one of two things. The first, and least concerning, is caused by artificial interference with the region. For instance, non-permitted mining of dark matter in deep space, or the unlicensed destruction of entire moons or planets for various nefarious purposes. These are local problems with no universal impact.

The second, is a shift in the stability of this particular universe. A far more serious concern with implications for the entire multiverse. The only way I can understand the multiverse is to imagine it as a gathering of bubbles or foam. Each bubble, or universe, is distinct, yet at the same time forms part of the structure of its neighbours. If one bubble collapses, the entire foam structure is altered. In response to the violent collapse of a single universe, many others collapse in what can become a catastrophic chain reaction. So, there are teams like us keeping a metaphorical eye on things.

Rosy and I are good at our job, so it's a surprise the Authorities have given us a new project we're not at all qualified for. Our new task is to inspect a galaxy, which is producing more light than their models show it's capable of generating. This project is the most exciting thing that's happened to us in the last twenty space years.

As programmed, we emerge from the worm hole at the outer limit of the universe. I cast my mind outwards in my habitual, if always futile, attempt to contact another mind or find some sort of living organism. For the briefest moment there is nothing.

Then I feel it, just a tickle at first before awareness explodes through all my senses. There's a sentient mind and not just any mind, it's an Elf. He's reaching out to me, as eager to make contact as I am.

Our minds smash into each other and I'm swept with feelings of intense passion and desire. To add to the confusion Rosy is having her own issues. She's sensed pheromones and is broadcasting her need to mate. Somewhere, in the glistening bright jewel of the galaxy before us, is a spacecraft with a male team.

I've never encountered the mind of a fabled Fire Elf before. It's overwhelming and all manner of hormones are released into my blood stream on instinct. My poor shrivelled, inert body hasn't felt such sensations for such a long time, I've almost forgotten what desire feels like.

Rosy bucks in her harness, triggering almost every alarm. I can't withhold my blast of sensations from the spacecraft. I'm terrified the Authorities will yank us back through the worm hole.

Silence.

Outside my pod I see smoke. The filters prevent me from enjoying the metallic odour of electronics melting. Just like in my fantasy, the Fire Elf has burnt out the circuitry. I can still breathe, and my visual monitors allow me to see outside the spacecraft, but every other system is dead. Hysteria bubbles up in my mind as I realise that Rosy and I are free from the Authorities. I try to laugh but the tubes prevent it.

Rosy is moving us through the galaxy tracking her mate. She doesn't move in her usual linear fashion, instead, we flit between solar systems. I had no idea she could move this way. I hadn't understood the horror of her confinement, it's been worse than my own.

I now know where the extra light is coming from. It's him – my Fire Elf. He lights the way, drawing us in. Suns burn hotter and whiter than they should in front of us, then expand into red giants as we leave them behind, their energy spent. It would be simpler for Rosy to follow the blazing stars, if only she could see. I'd guide her if she'd let me, but her mind is overwhelmed with the need to procreate. She's lost to me.

We're getting closer, I can feel him probing through my memories and thoughts. He's powerful and I can't resist. The intensity of his exploration is almost painful, like being too close to a flame. I have no idea who he is and how he came to be here. He gives me nothing, and yet knows all my secrets. If I could, I'd howl in frustration.

Our destination looms – a tiny solar system near the centre of the galaxy. The little sun pulses like a beacon. My heart is almost bursting as it pounds. A mixture of fear and desire releases a potent mixture of hormones into my bloodstream. Rosy surges on, flitting across vast expanses of space in the blink of an eye.

The violence of our arrival is shocking. We collide.

I can't escape the flood of images and feelings he pours into my mind. In a moment I know him. He is Lucilius – all fire and passion. The Authorities didn't understand his talents and underestimated him. He and Gilvus, his Space-Canary, escaped on their first mission. They've been here for over a hundred space years.

Touched with the madness of being isolated and constrained for too long, Lucilius entertained himself by manipulating the light in the galaxy around them. All this time, they've stayed hidden from the Authorities. Waiting for us – waiting for Rosy and me.

Rosy and Gilvus don't pause. They take up their ritualised mating dance. Twirling their bodies around each other they flit through space.

Harnessed to them Lucilius and I are dragged along. The hulls of our spacecraft clash and grind against each other.

In our minds we see one another as we were. He's golden skinned with flashing amber eyes. His flame-red hair dances around his face. He reaches for me. I wrap my pale slender body around his, my platinum tresses entwine us as his fire melts into my ice-blue eyes.

Minds open, we merge with Rosy and Gilvus. Our very cells disperse to join their amorphous swirl of pink and yellow. Our desire amplifies their need, and they respond. Bodies entwine and tangle, meld and re-combine as we consummate our union. Our tortured souls and bodies writhe in rapture.

Desire for the slow burn of bliss tempers our urge to reach completion. We probe and stroke, lick and thrust, grasp and bite with deliberate restraint, holding back the eruption for as long as possible. The ecstasy of our minds and bodies tipping over the edge into wave after wave of unified orgasm is almost more than our broken bodies can bear.

Time and space stand still. Tangled, stunned and exhausted we spiral through space.

Rosy disturbs our repose to scatter her fertilised eggs. We shudder with her as waves of pure pleasure flow through us. We're spent and complete. Our entire lives have led to this, there can be no more.

Like moths to a flame, we plunge into the closest sun.

THE UNWILLING PRINCESS

Renee stood astride the Suicide Rock staring down into the twisting mists. The tips of her braids flicked as the savage wind and pelting rain tore at her. The name of the rock was a misnomer, few people had used it for suicidal purposes. It was, instead, a place to meet with the dead. Once a year, on the anniversary of their death, the departed would rise from the mists to commune with their loved ones. Renee waited for Lily.

One year ago, on her birthday, Lily had tripped over Skrat and tumbled off the castle ramparts. She'd died on impact. In her grief and rage, Renee had thrown Skrat after her lover and the devilish cat had died as well.

Today was the first chance Renee had to speak to Lily since the terrible argument, which had sent Lily to the ramparts in anger. Nothing would have stopped Renee from the treacherous ascent of the strange rock. She'd outwitted the Queen's guards and escaped the castle. Not even the tempest could diminish her need to speak once more with her lover.

The Suicide Rock had sat over the edge of the ravine long before her people had come to this land and built their castle. Its surface was smooth and glossy with few handholds- – no weapon or tool they'd tried had made any impact on it. The red rock sat, implacable and unique, in a landscape of browns and greens.

There was no lore to how the Suicide Rock worked. It did or it didn't. The person you sought appeared, or they did not. So far, Renee had tried calling, chanting and singing. Still, Lily refused to appear. Tired, wet and cold Renee sunk to her knees and wept bitter tears of defeat.

"You always were too impatient, my sweet."

The voice was unmistakeable. Renee lifted her head, eyes wide open in disbelief. Hovering before her was the clear shape and form of Lily, not solid, but without doubt, Lily. Renee was disconcerted and a little delighted that Lily was naked. It made sense, clothes had no soul, but it made the ache of her loss sharpen.

"You look dreadful, my love. Are you not well?"

Renee swiped away the tears and rain with the back of her hand.

"I've missed you so much, Lily. I don't know what to do without you."

"Do your duty. For once in your life, do what you must do for your people."

Renee scrambled to her feet and stood ramrod straight. Why was Lily speaking to her this way? She'd expected death to soften the views of the woman she'd loved for most of her life. Renee's fists clenched white at her sides and the words came out with more venom than she'd meant.

"My duty? I will not marry that short, bald, sorry excuse for a duke just to appease Mother. My child-bearing days are long gone, there is absolutely no point to the union."

Lily started to drift apart and swirl with the winds.

"Wait, wait. Come back," Renee wailed. "I'm sorry. I'm sorry."

"Why do you continue to defy the queen, even after I've gone, Princess?"

"What else can I do? I never wanted this life. I never wanted to be a princess and to become queen. If she wants a successor, she'll have to marry someone herself. I only want to be with you, my love."

Renee flung herself forward, arms wide to embrace her lover for eternity.

At that moment, Skrat appeared mid-air between Lily and Renee. Lily's palms, solid and raised to stop Renee's fall, instead connected with the evil cat. Skrat's soul was pushed into Renee. Delighted at the result, the cat forced the unwilling princess' soul from her body.

Howling in horror, Lily and Renee hovered long enough to realise the deception, then dissolved into the wind. Balanced on the edge of

Suicide Rock, Skrat watched as their forms returned to the twisting mists below.

Unlike Princess Renee, Skrat had great ambitions to be queen. Lily's fall had been no accident, although the cat hadn't expected to be tossed after her with such violence. Still, it had all worked out in the end – she would be queen within days.

With as much cat-like grace as a 48-year-old woman's body would allow, Skrat leapt down from Suicide Rock and headed home. Like the princess, she was determined there would be no marriage on her way to the throne, although she did have an itch to scratch. Maybe she'd take as a lover the nice guard who'd fed her pieces of chicken on cold winter mornings? A purr thrummed in her throat.

Skrat sauntered back to the castle with murder on her mind.

HER HUSBAND

The woman prayed for her husband every day.
She prayed to Tangaroa.
Her husband came home safe from the sea.
She prayed to Rongomātāne.
Her husband came home safe from the fields.
She prayed to Tūmatauenga.
Her husband came home safe from war.
Under the cover of darkness, she prayed to Hinenuitepō.
Her husband woke up every morning.

• • • •

The woman changed her approach.
She spoke to the kererū.
Telling of her husband's anger.
She spoke to the tūī.
Whispering the toxic words her husband used.
She spoke to the pīwakawaka.
Explaining her fear of her husband.
Under the cover of darkness, she spoke to the ruru.
Showing the bruises inflicted by her husband.

• • • •

Tānemahuta listened to the songs of his forest.
When the widow-maker fell, her husband was buried deep.

• • • •

The woman planted miro.
Berries for the kererū.
The woman planted kōwhai.

Nectar for the tūī.
The woman planted korokio.
Insects for the pīwakawaka.
Under the cover of darkness, she carved cavities in thick tree trunks.
Safe nesting holes for ruru.

• • • •

The woman flourished in her forested garden.
Free from her husband.

THE GROTESQUE WARS

Skulls crunched underfoot as Fredegund strode through the cavernous hall. Thousands had died over the ages, their detached heads brought here, where they lay piled in varying stages of decay. Here and there a remnant of long-dried flesh clung to white bone, and tangles of matted hair twisted around detached mandibles. These were the only hints the owners of the bones had once lived and breathed. No mourners came to this place in search of lost loved ones. The skulls remained orphaned from their bodies and lives – staring at each other in vacant death until crushed under each other's weight.

Despite her haste she paused to admire the dreadfulness of her surroundings and her heart swelled with pride. She recalled the epic battles won against the Horde, who had risen against her and those she protected. Her face and body bore many scars, but *her* head remained attached to her body.

Twin long-knives, sheathed in the leather harness nestled between her wings. Despite years of disuse, the blades remained bright, their edges ground and polished to slice at the lightest touch. She hoped she wouldn't need to draw them today.

It'd been eighty-three years since Clovis had last awoken, and then only for the time it took to help her turn the tide against the Horde. Once the battle had tilted in their favour, he'd left her to finish the rout. Ever since, he'd sat motionless at the edge of the roof on the tallest tower of the chateau. The largest of the grotesques, his formidable presence struck terror into any who raised their eyes in his direction.

Fredegund stopped and listened. There it was – the distinctive crack of the slow splintering of stone. She sniffed the stale air, sorting through the tangled odours of desiccated flesh, crushed bone, rat shit, pulverised cockroaches, and dried blood, until she found it. Fresh ground masonry mixed with male musk. It was almost time. The moons would soon align, and he would rise for the rut. The others would follow.

Fredegund took a deep breath and held it for a moment before allowing the air to escape in a steady, controlled exhalation. She lifted her right wing and ran an appraising eye along the bony leading edge to the silver tipped spur on the articulated joint at the apex. The wing extended to its full span, stretching the leathery membrane and supporting cartilage. She checked both wings for any unhealed nicks or cuts – there were none. A single beat lifted her from her feet. Satisfied, she settled and tucked the appendages behind her once again.

With her tail held high, Fredegund strode on through the drifts of skulls, towards the giant double doorway leading to the courtyard. As Guardian, it was her job to be nearby when Clovis transitioned, to protect him and the others.

· · · ·

Despite all her years of training, Martha felt nervous. Today, Romanus would decide whether she, or one of the others, would become the Charm. Only four, from the twenty who had been bred for the quest, had made it to this point. Martha would be the final aspirant to enter his chamber.

The sun was just setting when they collected her. As she was led across the courtyard the sky flushed orange red. A good sign.

Romanus sat on his great chair – his face devoid of expression. The door shut, leaving them alone in his chamber. He said nothing, just stared. Martha willed herself to relax and maintain the passive and pleasant expression she had learned in childhood.

With the slightest movement of a finger, Romanus signalled she should twirl. Mid-turn, Martha released the knot holding her covering in place. The sheer fabric fluttered away to pool at her feet, leaving her naked when she faced the appraiser once again. She caught the change in the size of his pupils and the flare of his nostrils. Pressing home her advantage she flicked soft red waves of hair over her shoulders to expose her breasts.

She lowered her eyelids, but not so much that she broke eye contact with Romanus. Still silent, he waved her forward. With three slow steps Martha complied, then sank to her knees at his feet. Her heart fluttered to be so close to him.

"May I please you, my Lord?"

Romanus cleared his throat as if to speak but nodded instead.

Slipping her hands between the flaps of his deep-blue satin robe Martha was relieved to discover he wore nothing underneath. There would be no awkward fumbling with fastenings to interfere with her performance. She rewarded him with her most dazzling smile while her fingertips trailed up his inner thighs towards her prize. She wrapped her fingers around his shaft, it stiffened in her palm.

Martha leaned in between his now spread knees. Not waiting for his hand on her head she leaned forward to hover over his tip, so close he must feel her breath. When her tongue made soft contact, she was gratified by his moan.

She licked and sucked at him as if she was lapping up the final traces of honey from her fingers. He wrapped his hands in her hair and moved his hips against her. The deeper and faster he thrust the harder she sucked. Leaving one hand wrapped around his base she slid the other down to grasp his balls, squeezing them in time with his lunges.

Lord Romanus yanked her head back. Martha's stomach lurched. Had she failed? Frozen in shock, her mouth still forming a circle, she stared into his eyes.

A dark expression shadowed his face. It was neither anger nor disgust. Was that what lust looked like?

Martha knew she had won. He would take her and release the Charm.

Romanus lifted her from the floor, carried her to his bed and tossed her down. The stark white sheets felt smooth and cool against her skin.

He threw off his robe of office. Martha took in his magnificence, her heart pounding in anticipation.

A man of superior stature and strength, Romanus had beaten off over a hundred challengers to gain his position. His word was law. Scars traced the muscular contours of his chest to create designs of haphazard disorder. Arms and shoulders also bore the signatures of violent conflict. The lines of his visage were hard.

He planted a knee between her open thighs and slid a thick finger over her cleft.

"Are you prepared for the gratification?"

"I am ready, my Lord. My life has been dedicated to the privilege of receiving your beneficence. I am honoured to surrender myself to you. I am your vassal, my Lord. Use me as you will." The words of the pledge issued forth without hesitation. She had practised day and night for the last year.

He was meant to reply, 'On your blood, you will be the Charm. Mine to have and command. Devoted to my service and desires.' He didn't. Instead, he pushed her legs further apart and pushed himself into her.

Her training had not taken her this far, but the Matrons had described what was about to happen. Yet, their description was not quite right. It hurt. Martha gasped. He groaned and a sheen of sweat coated his brow.

"I can't...I have to..."

He didn't finish his sentence. Martha cried out at the burst of pain as he thrust his full length into her. This was not the ecstasy the Matrons had described. She flung her head sideways so her Lord wouldn't see her tears of pain and distress. He buried his teeth in her exposed neck and bit hard.

Romanus arched his back, shuddered and held his thrust deep inside her wounded cunt. Spent, he collapsed his full weight onto her with a final grunt. His drool trickled down her neck. It took all of Martha's self-control not to beat him off her.

When his breathing calmed, Romanus withdrew. His usual disdain reinstated, he climbed from the bed, retrieved his robe and strode from the room. Martha lay unmoving, tears wetting the sheet beneath her cheek.

Several moments later, the Matrons appeared. They clucked with delight over her virgin blood smeared on the sheet, then draped Martha in the red covering of the Charm. She sat in the docile manner of her training while they primped her hair and applied ceremonial paints and powders to her face.

Nothing in her expression or behaviour betrayed the bitterness in her heart. The Charm had not been released. Her entire life had been a lie.

• • • •

The chateau sat atop a rock formation towering above the surrounding countryside. A single road wound up from the plains to the outer gateway. Bands of iron reinforced the hardwood gate, which was thicker than the width of Fredegund's shoulders. The ramparts had crumbled in places but remained intact. The fortress almost impenetrable.

There was no memory of how long the chateau had stood. The Kings and Queens of old had turned to dust millennia ago, their mausoleums the only reminders of their dominion over the invading Horde.

The chateau had become one of the few remaining sanctuaries for Fredegund's kind. Here, the stone-like creatures could rest without constant threat of destruction at the hateful hands of the Horde. As Guardian, she was charged with protecting the vulnerable gathering of slumbering grotesques. It was a solitary life, but one to which she had become accustomed.

From the top of the ramparts, Fredegund gazed out towards the blurred lights from the city of the Horde. In the early days it had been a collection of flimsy tents, then had come the wooden shacks, followed by stone buildings. Now, towers and spires had begun to appear. A permanent veil of smoke shrouded the spreading city. The sight filled her with dread. She turned away. Nothing good could come from that place.

Right now, danger was much closer at hand. Not only was Clovis well into his awakening, but a few of the putti were also starting to crack their stone shells. She did not need those evil little troublemakers aggravating an already inflamed Clovis. Even without their interference it would take all her efforts to prevent Clovis from killing Guntrum and the other males before they awoke for combat.

The first moon began its slow creep from below the horizon, bathing the grey stone walls of the chateau in a soft pink glow. The second moon would soon follow. Fredegund had no time to spare on worries. It was time for her to play her part in the oncoming drama. She jumped onto the parapet and ran its length towards the nearest tower. With an easy leap she cleared the distance between the two and used her forward momentum to scale the sheer wall of the tower without the need for flight.

Launching from between the frozen forms of two lower echelon grotesques, she landed on the roof of the hall at a full run. She sprinted along the tiles of the ridge cap, not pausing when she heard the giggles of the almost mobile putti poised over the eaves. Stretching her wings, she leapt into the air. In three beats she reached Clovis – the last of his stone veneer crumbled and fell with a clatter to the courtyard far below.

Clovis inhaled, re-inflating his lungs as the silver light of the second moon touched his exposed skin. He roared, raising his arms and face to the night sky, wings stretched to their full span. The burst of flame illuminated the entire chateau.

Even Fredegund trembled in awe at his magnificence.

"Clovis. I am Fredegund, the Guardian. Remember me." Her voice rose, powerful and commanding.

Turning his terrible regard in her direction, the vertical slits of his pupils widened. Clovis tipped his head sideways to stare down at her. His nostrils flared and his forked tongue flicked out through thick lips to taste the air.

"I remember you, Guardian. Feed me."

Stung he'd used her honorific, and not her name, Fredegund hesitated in her response.

Clovis didn't ask twice. Using his tail, he knocked her off her feet and loomed over her.

Realising her mistake, and the danger she'd put them in, Fredegund rolled away and flipped herself back to her feet.

"Fly Covis. Fly towards the rising moons." She instructed.

She didn't bother to watch Clovis take to the air. He would need a fresh kill to sustain him through the challenges ahead. If he was fortunate, and he should be, he would find unguarded livestock in the surrounding fields. Otherwise, he'd have to fly the moderate distance to the forest.

Fredegund swooped across the courtyard to the next tallest tower. To the annoyed chittering of the gathering putti, she was ready when Guntrum wrapped his muscular arms around her torso and tried to bite off her head.

Throughout the night, the grotesque warriors awoke in the order corresponding to strength and position in their structured society. It wasn't a fair system, the weaker males had less time to feed and were at higher risk of attack by the putti, but it maintained order.

It was almost dawn when it happened. A flurry of awakenings occurred, too many for Fredegund to help. Without her there to send him to the fields, one of the grotesques succumbed to the call of the putti. The little nudes surrounded him, giggling and petting him with their chubby little hands until his hunger got the better of him. He grabbed for one of them.

The putti's sweet smiles stretched to reveal rows of sharp pointed teeth. They tore the young grotesque to shreds. Putti swarmed from all over the chateau to gorge on their prey. Chunks of flesh landed on the flagstones below with sickening slaps.

Fredegund shut her eyes, but she couldn't block out the crunching of bones, tearing of flesh and slurping of blood. Nothing remained of the grotesque when they'd finished. Even the flagstones were licked clean.

Fredegund dropped to the lowest corbel to help the final and youngest of the males to emerge from his slumber. He would have little time to feast but it wouldn't matter. He was far too small to compete with Clovis for the right to fly their queen. It was her role to help him survive until he could. Her tail thrashed at any putti who came within striking distance. The silver spike that adorned the tip of her tail kept the pack of fat, smiling predators at bay.

She helped him struggle out of his shell of cracked mortar. "What is your name?"

"I am Audon," he said with a crooked smile. "Thanks for helping me."

"I am Fredegund, the Guardian, my purpose is to protect and assist you. You need to fly as fast as you're able and feed. I usually keep them for myself, but there are lots of fat trout in the dark river pool just outside the forest. Go now"

"Thank you, Fredegund." He stretched his wings and shot into the air.

Fredegund smiled. Audon was small, and no match for any of his rivals, but if she favoured him, he'd grow faster. And for some reason, Fredegund did favour him.

• • • •

Martha now occupied a strange position. Although still a servant, with precious little freedom, she was worshipped by the Horde as a living goddess. With her designation as the Charm came luxury. Her new bedchamber was large and well-furnished, the fabrics sumptuous silks, satins and the finest cottons, all dyed red.

Upon arrival in her new rooms – still dazed and confused – Martha had been fed by the Matrons. Their attitude towards their previous ward had changed only a little. Though more respectful, no longer slapping or pinching her when she was slow to react, they still prodded and berated her when she only picked at the food. Martha forced herself to swallow several mouthfuls of the poached trout and a few spears of fresh asparagus. She also managed a morsel of soft cheese and two plump figs drizzled in honey. Satisfied, the Matrons had pressed a crystal goblet of rich red liquid into her hand and left.

Alone, she stood at the large window and stared at the chateau. It thrust up from the surrounding plains to disrupt the flat horizon with violent lines. She'd never seen it in this way before. Bathed in the pink light of the first moon it was almost beautiful. Nothing at all like the grey and blackened citadel of terror she'd been taught to fear and loathe. Maybe that, too, had been a lie.

Her mind had been filled with heretical thoughts since her investiture in Romanus' chamber. If Romanus had not been able to awaken the Charm, what other untruths had she been taught? Her hand shook and she gulped a mouthful of the red spirit from the goblet. The fiery liquid burned its way to her stomach, making her eyes water.

Far away, over the chateau there was an enormous flash of fire. The goblet in Martha's slipped from her fingers and a blood red stain pooled around at her feet. She pressed her body against the chill of the window glass, but all she could feel was the heat from the flame caress her skin and ignite her desire.

The monster was awake.

The flame extinguished. She sank to her knees, her forehead still resting against the window. Slipping her hand beneath her silken covering, Martha sought the taboo territory between her thighs. She explored herself in a way forbidden to her. Even now, as the Charm, she didn't think she'd escaped punishment if the Matrons walked in to find her in this flagrant act of self-pleasure.

Amongst her soft folds of flesh, she discovered a firm little nub. Touching it sent jolts of delight radiating through her body. Her body tensed and her breath caught. Martha's first orgasm flooded her body and mind with ecstasy. Not caring if she was discovered, she cried in jubilation.

Slumped and gasping for breath before the darkened vista, Martha searched her memory for any hint of what she'd just experienced. But the lessons had been clear. The Charm would feel the ecstasy at her investiture. How then could the awakening of the evil creature, signalled by the flame, elicit this response from her flesh when her own Lord left her disgusted and in pain?

A second flame disrupted the darkness of her view and thoughts, and again desire swept through her. Flames flared throughout the hours of darkness. Somewhere in the night she lost herself in the revelation of her own passion.

She was no longer Martha – the Charm had been released.

After the sun had cast its rays on the world she crawled into her bed and slept without dreams.

The Matrons came for her when the sun hovered just shy of its zenith. They bustled into her room, tutting at the stain on the floor and the torn covering crumpled at the foot of the bed. Incensed at their impertinence, the Charm sat upright, her eyes aflame with fury.

"I am the Charm. You will bow before me." The voice was strong and of a deeper register than Martha had possessed.

The Matrons stopped their fussing and stared at her wide-eyed before dropping to their knees one after another.

"That's better. You," she said pointing at the nearest, "run me a bath. The rest of you withered old crones will leave me."

The Matrons scrambled and scuttled out of the room. The Charm lay back in the luxury of her bed. She stretched and drank in the view towards the chateau. He would be sitting on the tallest tower sleeping in the sun, perhaps facing the city. Was he looking at her? Her cheeks flushed.

The room filled with the aroma of spiced oils carried on the steam from her bath. Glorying in her newfound power, the Charm strolled naked across the room. She stepped into the bath, lowering herself into the delicious warmth with a sigh of pleasure. The attending Matron turned away.

"Bring me a beverage, crone. The bitter, black one."

"You mean coffee, my Lady?"

"I am no lady," she shouted, glaring at the unfortunate Matron. "I am the Charm. Yes...the beverage you call coffee. And make it sweet, little insect."

The Matron crawled backwards from the room. By the time she returned with a pot of sweetened coffee, the Charm had finished bathing and stood before the window, drying herself with a soft towel. The Matron served the coffee then retreated to the corner of the room where she sat on her knees with her head bowed.

The Charm settled herself into the cushioned comfort of an armchair. She inhaled the coffee's rich aroma, then took a sip. She closed her eyes and swirled the bitter sweetness around her tongue.

She snapped her fingers, pointed at her hairbrush and beckoned the Matron over. The Charm sipped her coffee while the brush massaged her scalp with rhythmic strokes. The Matron continued to brush until her hair shone and lay in loose waves that tumbled to her waist.

Her coffee finished, the Charm stood and made for the door. "I will now see Romanus."

"Charm, do not forget your covering." The Matron scuttled across the room to snatch a fresh red covering from the closet.

"I am the Charm. This is what I am. This is how I am. I have no need of your coverings and your paints."

The woman dropped the offending fabric as if it was on fire and prostrated herself on the floor.

"Of course, Charm. You are glorious as you are. I am blessed to serve you."

• • • •

Fredegund slept for over half of the sunlight hours of the day. She woke feeling strong and ready. Having feasted before the awakening, she would not feed again for several days. She dropped from her perch to the floor, walked to the courtyard and stretched her wings in the sun to soak in the warmth.

She checked to be sure the males had all made it back from their hunt to slumber in the sun. They would need their strength this night. She was intrigued to see that Audon was the only one not in his rightful position. He'd taken the place the dead male had left free. In doing so, Audon had raised himself above two of his elders. A bold move.

With an easy leap Fredegund took to the air. She mounted in slow, lazy circles, taking the time to inspect her charges. She also made sure the putti had retreated to their roof-edges and were up to no mischief. Satisfied all was as it should be with the awoken, she flew to the Queen's spire and landed on the small balcony next to the frozen form of Brunhilda.

Fredegund gave her full attention to her queen. She ran her practiced hands over every curve of the stone surface, searching for any signs of damage. She admired the curvaceous beauty of her mother's full round belly, thick thighs, and wide hips. Her fingers drifted across the pendulous fullness of the three sets of teats. Despite the passage of time, she remembered the sweet, rich, creaminess of the milk she'd suckled alongside the others of her litter. A rare litter of females, she'd killed them all to become Guardian.

Her inspection complete, and having found no damage, she flew to the iron lightning rod at the highest point of the Chateau. Perched atop the rod, she spotted the army of the Horde camped below the Chateau.

The Horde had set up their temporary camp at the foot of the rock formation. They would not attack tonight. They would watch in fear then attack with the sun. The formula never changed. No need for panic, this was a conflict with no beginning and no end. The grotesques and the Horde were destined to repeat their battles century after century. She stroked the handles of her long-knives. This time would be no different.

In the late afternoon, Fredegund circled out to check on the Horde camp. She was careful to remain well above the range of their archers. All was as it had always been, with one exception. A single red pavilion had been erected at the base of the track leading to the Chateau. Fredegund was puzzled. Why had the Horde blocked their only access to the Chateau with the structure? She could see no immediate threat so returned to her preparations.

At twilight the males began dropping from their perches to collect handfuls of fire-rocks from the piles Fredegund had arranged around the courtyard. She kept a close eye on them, ready to intervene with extreme violence if any disputes broke out. The pull of the moons would not be in full effect until they both rose above the horizon. The putti were already gathered into chattering gangs.

This was the most dangerous time, the time before the combat. Fredegund was ready for anything.

There were a couple of minor scuffles amongst the lower echelon males, but no need for her intervention. They were soon sitting back in their positions chewing on small rocks until they were reduced to stones small enough to swallow. It wasn't quite dark enough to see the sparks as they chewed. The males would hold the stones in their crops to ignite their flames.

Fredegund looked at Audon. He'd collected a large pile of fire-rocks, demonstrating his intention to survive more than a few challenges. It was going to be an interesting evening. Before the sky darkened, she, too, dipped down to scoop up a handful of fire-rocks, chewing them she flew to her perch on the lightening rod.

When the last ray of sunshine slid below the horizon Fredegund stretched out her wings, tipped back her head and clenched her throat. She felt the flare as the flame burst forth with a roar. She could feel all eyes upon her – the grotesques, the putti and the Horde far below. In this moment she held them all in her thrall.

"Tonight, the twin moons rise as one." Her voice boomed. "Through their power you too will rise, my brothers. You will rise in combat to seek the strongest one. Like the moons you will rise in pairs to fight in single combat. I will show no mercy to any who stray." The long-knives in her hands radiating their own light against the blackness of the sky. "Brunhilda, our Queen, awaits her victor."

The final echo of her voice disappeared across the plains and the twin moons broke the far horizon side-by-side, the pink and silver bleeding together to cast a pale mauve glow across the landscape.

Fredegrund launched straight up into the air with a final command. "Fly, my brothers. Fly."

The air filled with movement and sound. Every awakened winged creature inhabiting the chateau took flight.

The first eager challengers flung themselves into combat. Clovis and Guntrum drew away from each other, taking up positions on opposite sides of the chateau. They had no need to participate in the early skirmishes between the lower echelons. Other than a chance to improve their position in the hierarchy, all the early winners would gain for themselves was another challenge. Fredegund spotted Audon, he too kept himself clear of the pack.

The putti harried the early combatants without mercy, pulling their tails, grabbing their wings and hanging from their backs. The challenges were never meant to be fatal or cause major injury. Rather they were a show of strength and virility. The putti though, craving grotesque flesh, did all they could to put the adversaries into harm's way and expose them to accidental injury.

Audon made his first challenge in the fourth round of duels. Gararic, a mid-echelon grotesque, had already survived two encounters and remained strong. Audon ducked and feinted the flame attacks of his larger foe, then responded with his own burst of flame strong enough to cause his opponent to falter in his flight.

The hardened edge of Audon's tail caught Gararic in the temple. A gang of putti pounced on the stunned grotesque, ripping holes in his wings. He crumpled and plunged towards the ground. Audon threw himself into a dive, reaching to grab his opponent mid-fall, he was driven back by the putti defending their spoils of war.

Neither Fredegund, nor any of the other males, sought to intervene to save Gararic. The putti, for all their unpleasantness, had no lesser right to life than the grotesques or even the Horde gathered on the plain. They were all part of the same cyclic ritual, their roles defined and necessary to maintain the established balance of their domains.

Fredegund was surprised by Audon's reaction to the accident. Instead of celebrating his easy victory and seeking another challenge, he flew down to hover next to Gararic's roost, but didn't take it. He'd already gained a significant boost in his status, lifting himself from a wall decoration to the top of a medium-height tower. An impressive feat for such a young grotesque.

Distracted, she almost missed Guntrum's first combat.

He was challenged by Merovech, a middle echelon victor. Guntrum's burst of flame caught his challenger off-guard and sent him tumbling sideways. To his credit, the out-classed Merovech regained his wings before any of the putti were able to take advantage of his error. More cautious now the challengers were larger and stronger, the putti flitted close-by, laughing and giggling, but taking care to avoid the grotesque's tails slicing the air like knives.

Guntrum was larger, faster and stronger than his opponent and the duel short-lived. Merovech retreated to his new roost, two positions higher than the one he had vacated.

By the time the moons neared their apex, the time of their strongest influence, only two undefeated grotesques remained on high – Guntrum and Clovis. They hovered, each waiting for the other to challenge. The hysterical laughter of the putti signalled something unusual was taking place.

Audon burst through the cloud of chattering putti, dragging a collective gasp from those already defeated, and came face to face with Guntrum. Now Fredegund understood why Audon had not settled into his new roost, hovering close by instead. Grotesques who had not claimed a roost remained free to challenge.

Guntrum laughed as the youngest grotesque hovered in front of him. His laugh turned to a howl when Audon flipped on his wing and encircled the veteran in a ring of fire. To avoid Guntrum's return blast of flame, Audon eschewed tradition and dipped sideways, weaving his way between towers and skimming rooftops. Those already at their roosts were sent skittering high into the air to avoid the low-level aerial combat.

• • • •

The Charm watched the grotesques with fascination. Despite the years of indoctrination at the hands of the Matrons, she did not find the grotesques terrifying or dreadful. To her eye they were magnificent creatures of enormous strength and passion, traits she found attractive.

She resisted the temptation to pleasure herself and set off up the path. It took half the night to climb her way up the mountainside, all the while aware of the battles taking place overhead. She had no need to camouflage her approach. Not a single creature on the plains was looking her way. All eyes were riveted on the drama in the sky above the chateau. She had never felt safer than she did trekking up the side of the mountain, naked and alone.

The Charm had almost reached the massive wooden gates when events changed overhead. Even to her inexperienced eye this new challenge was different from the rest. With a mixture of admiration and lust, she watched the small challenger draw his larger opponent down amongst the lower structures of the chateau. As the foes flew low along the ramparts, she ducked to avoid the searing heat from a blast of flame. When she lifted her gaze, the Charm found the eyes of the one she sought.

Her heart pounded – she drank in his glory. The muscles of his legs were defined with such sharpness she could count them if she wished, while those of his arms bulged and stretched in magnificent rivalry. He sank towards her, vast wings blocking all else from view. Although his face was twisted into a fearsome grimace, his eyes...her thoughts trailed away as she surrendered to his eyes.

With the barest movement of air, he landed in front of her, crouching until they were eye to eye.

"I am the Charm."

"I am Clovis." His voice sounded like rocks tumbling in a flooded river.

The Charm lifted her hand to cup his face, "The twin moons have led me to you. I am yours, Clovis."

Her fingers rippled over the corrugated muscles of his midriff. Before her hand could sink lower, he grabbed her wrist in an iron grasp. His free hand slid down her spine, over the curve of her buttocks and pushed between her thighs. She sank into his grasp. Then they were airborne.

The sensation was more than she had imagined. The ground rushed away. The waves of her hair whipped around their bodies. The odours of rocks, lichens, fire and flesh faded along with the chittering of the putti and the guttural cries of his clan as Clovis lifted her higher and closer to the twins.

The Charm wrapped her legs around him. She brought her mouth to his, sliding her tongue between lush lips to explore within. His forked tongue twisted and twirled around hers. Clovis lifted her by the hips to sit on his shoulders, his face between her thighs. Any fear at such a vulnerable perch at their altitude was obliterated by the magic of his tongue. He probed and sucked. The Charm grasped his head and groaned. Waves of ecstasy surged through her. The Charm arched her back and fell.

Powerless to save herself, she could only stare up at her lover. He watched for a moment, then folded his wings and speared into a dive, at the last moment he swooped. The Charm welcomed him with open arms and legs. He penetrated her as their bodies crashed together. She raked her nails down his back to the base of his tail – he arched in reflex then thrust. Their hips crushed together. She bit onto his lower lip. His fingers bruised her flesh. Releasing his lip, she tipped her head to expose the base of her neck. His teeth latched onto the soft skin. With a growl, Clovis unleashed his lust. Their ascent towards the twin moons faltered.

Devoid of love or affection, they fucked. Their grinding rhythm turned frenzied. Thrashing together, they hovered. Grunts rose to orgasmic howls. Clovis raised his head and roared with a flame that outshone the light of the twin moons.

They fluttered earthwards towards the chateau. With her final shred of energy, the Charm pointed towards her red pavilion at the base of the path. Clovis altered his course without question, landing with such care the canvas didn't even flutter. She led him inside to the softness of her bed, where, bodies tangled, they fell asleep.

The Charm's slumber was so profound she did not hear or feel her limbs pushed aside as massive iron cuffs clamped shut on her lover's wrists and ankles.

• • • •

Audon's unexpected victory over Guntrum was the first sign of trouble. His unorthodox approach to their duel flummoxed his larger, stronger and more experienced adversary. In using the towers and battlements of the chateau as obstacles, Audon's smaller size and agility gave him the advantage. He flicked around a corner with a spin, catching Guntrum with the full force of his tail smashing him against the stone wall of the hall. The swarm of putti who trailed them at a discrete distance dived without hesitation.

This time, Audon was prepared. He prevented their attack by shielding Guntrum with his wings, his tail thrashing in all directions. Foiled, the putti retreated. Guntrum ceded the battle and flew to a lower roost. Humiliated, he didn't wait to see the outcome of the final duel. He tucked himself into his sleep position and proceeded to re-petrify.

Distracted by the unexpected duel. Fredegund didn't notice Clovis had disappeared. She blamed herself for everything that followed. She was the Guardian, charged to prepare for this night and protect the combatants. In not paying more attention to the unusual red pavilion, she had exposed the grotesques to an unprecedented act of treachery.

When Clovis soared skywards with the human woman wound around his body even the putti cried out in alarm. Fredegund gave brief chase, but he was too fast and powerful for her to pursue. It was too late to prevent the inevitable.

She also had other matters to deal with. Brunhilde had awoken and was bugling for her mate. Then, the victorious Audon flew to her side with anguished cries.

"I didn't mean to win, Guardian. I didn't mean to win. I'm sorry. What do I do? I don't know what to do."

"Well, you did win, Audon." Fredegund failed to keep the fury out of her voice. "Clovis is forfeit. You must fulfil your duty and take Brunhilda in flight."

"But Clovis was meant to fly with the Queen. I did not mean to win. I just wanted to try. I didn't mean to win."

"You should have thought of that earlier, Audon." Her voice rose to a shout. "Your Queen calls. Go to her."

To his credit, Audon did as he was instructed and flew to face his Queen. Brunhilda rose to her full glory, towering over the youth.

She snarled, "Where is my victor?"

"I am your victor, my Queen. I am Audon."

Brunhilda's laugh was a terrible thing. Her roar caused the putti to flee and the vanquished males to cower. Audon maintained his dignity in the face of the Queen's ridicule. Fredegund was impressed.

"You cannot fly me, tiny creature. You have neither the strength nor the stamina for my tastes."

Fredegund knew her mother spoke the truth. The youth could not fulfil his role. She swooped to place herself between them to prevent any violence.

"My Queen, my mother." She kept her voice soft. "Misfortune has fallen this night at the hands of the Horde. Raise your head and see for yourself. Clovis flies this night with a human woman. We have been deceived."

"I am fertile and ready to receive the seed of life into my wombs. Who will satisfy me if Clovis has fallen? This small creature who calls himself the victor is unworthy."

"He is worthy, my Queen. He vanquished Guntrum, who has retreated to stone in shame. Do not punish Audon for this travesty. The blame lies down there on the plain at the hands of the Horde." Fredegund pointed towards the canvas encampment. "They must pay."

"I need to be flown. Is there none who can take me?" Brunhilda's voice turned plaintive.

"Audon can satisfy your desire, but you will not be taken in flight this twin moons. Your wombs will remain empty this cycle."

Brunhilda sighed with resignation and beckoned for Audon to approach her. She lowered her massive frame to lie along the curve of the roofline and raised her tail. "Service me."

Fredegund retreated a short distance but stayed close enough to intervene if required. She was pleased to observe that Audon applied himself to his task with vigour. Understanding his Queen required release, he wasted no time. In another of his surprise manoeuvres he flicked his tail around and thrust it deep inside her, flicking and thrusting until she shouted in rapturous orgasm.

Fredegund could now focus on the events taking place high above them, where Clovis still flew the human woman. She watched the woman hurtle towards the ground only to be pierced by Clovis in his signature dive.

The twin moons were now at their full power.

Horrified, she watched the overhead dance to its conclusion. Then, instead of returning to the chateau, Clovis descended all the way down to the red pavilion at the edge of the horde's campsite.

Taking care to cast no shadow, Fredegund risked a silent, low glide over the camp. Her guts turned cold when the warriors crept from their hides and swarmed the red pavilion.

Clovis was captured. She had failed him.

Fredegund joined Audon and Brunhhilda atop the tallest tower. She was certain her face bore the same grim expression as theirs. Never had such a series of disasters befallen the grotesques on the night of the twin moons. The cycle of renewal had been broken. Lives had been lost, and Clovis had fallen to the Horde.

The sun broke through the gloom of the preceding night and with it a spark of hope ignited within Fredegund's belly.

"We must save him," she said.

"We cannot do it alone," Brunhilda said. "Our strongest are not with us. No offence, my little victor," she nodded at Audon, "but we are much reduced in strength."

"The putti will help us. This affects them as well," Audon said. "We don't need to fight the entire army of the Horde – we just need to find Clovis and free him."

"But we must punish the humans for their treachery. They have altered the balance of our world. Who knows what will transpire?" Fredegund released her fury by pulling her long-knives from their sheaths. She stood tall, sunlight flashing from the flaming blue steel. "Their blood must flow, and heads must roll in retribution."

"Guardian, my fierce daughter," Brunhilda's voice was soft, "you are magnificent, but I will not permit you to sacrifice those of us who remain for revenge. We will do as Audon suggests and free Clovis. If in the process we win a few human heads, then all the better, but it will not be our primary endeavour."

Fredegund knew her mother was right, but her bloodlust was strong, and she struggled with a desire to contradict the Queen's decision. Sheathing her knives, she breathed out her frustration.

"We'll fly when the sun reaches its zenith, and the shadows are at their smallest." She turned to Audon. "You should order one of the lower echelon males out to scout over the city. If we assume that Clovis is still alive, we need to know where he is being held or there will be no point in making an assault."

Audon looked at her. "Give orders?"

"You are the victor and consort to the Queen. So yes, give orders."

The small male bowed and took to the wing without further question.

Fredegund turned to her mother. "And you, our Queen, will summon the putti and make them understand what we expect from them." Without waiting for a response, Fredegund swooped down from the tower to explain the plan to the vanquished.

· · · ·

No matter how much the Charm raged, Romanus would neither see her nor permit her to leave her rooms. With the waning power of the twin moons, Martha felt the arrogance of the Charm slipping away. However, in its place a quiet, stubborn confidence remained.

She hadn't seen Clovis since his capture. By the time she had awoken, he was already shackled and gagged to prevent him flaming his captors. They had sliced the membranes of his wings to further disable him. She had screamed and lunged at the warriors who dared mutilate the lover of the Charm. Restrained by two guards, she had sworn her innocence and begged his forgiveness. Clovis had refused to look her way as he was dragged from the red pavilion.

From her window, Martha had a clear view into the city square far below. All morning men had been delivering timber by the cart load, each new load stacked onto the growing pile around the tall metal pole in the centre of the square. They were building a pyre.

Something caught her eye and she looked upwards. Her heart skipped a beat. Almost invisible against the glare of the mid-morning sun, a solitary winged creature flew towards the city.

Pressing her face against the smooth glass, Martha strained to watch the grotesque's approach. When it reached the square, it hovered for the briefest moment then flipped to fly fast towards the Chateau. Martha smiled.

She was still flattened against the window when the door to her rooms opened. Expecting her chosen Matron, she whirled to assault the woman with the tongue of the Charm. Those words failed to form. Romanus stood before her.

She wondered how she had ever revered this monster. Now, Martha could only see the putrescence beneath the façade of his handsome face.

"So, Charm. You subdued the beast by fucking him? That wasn't exactly our plan for you, but we thank you nevertheless."

She didn't argue when he instructed her to dress. She didn't resist when the Matrons painted and powdered her face. She didn't fight when the soldiers led her outside. She didn't cry. She didn't scream. Martha waited. The Charm waited. They would have their revenge.

Martha wasn't prepared for the sights, sounds and smells that assailed her when she was led into the square for the first time in her life. The throng of witnesses swayed towards her. She recoiled as the stench of rotten teeth, unwashed bodies, shit, piss and vomit filled her nostrils. Her stomach lurched. Shouts, insults, screeches, whistles and hoots echoed off the walls of the surrounding buildings, feeding back on themselves and rising in volume until her very skin hurt.

The silence, when it came, was almost as painful as the noise. Romanus entered the square behind her. The throng dropped to their knees with a singular rustle. Over the sea of backs, she at last saw Clovis. Her bones turned to water. She stumbled but was held upright by strong arms on either side.

Even mutilated, muzzled and restrained, Clovis was magnificent. Chained to the post atop the pyre, he held his head high, dignified in defeat. His shredded wings were pinned out either side of the heap of wood, while his broken tail lay limp behind him. His face betrayed no hint of pain.

Clovis' eyes bored into hers, tracking her while she was marched towards the pyre. Her tears, carved through the layers of paint and powder, cleansing and purging her shame. His nod filled her with courage.

Under the blaze of the midday sun the Charm was at her weakest, but Martha drew on every iota of available power. She shook free of the soldiers' grip and turned her fury on Romanus.

"I, the Charm, will kill you for this act of evil, Lord Romanus." She swept her arm out over the kneeling crowd, open-mouthed faces staring. "You have meddled with the natural order of the world and in doing so you have doomed these citizens to their death."

With strength, speed and agility beyond her human capacity, Martha seized a sword from the grip of the nearest soldier, bound up the pile of timber and slashed at the bindings holding her lover's muzzle in place.

Clovis tore his wings free from the spikes and wrapped them around her. His first flame burned the front rows of advancing soldiers and some of the surging crowd. Over the sounds of their screams Martha heard the unmistakable beat of wings.

The grotesques had arrived.

• • • •

Fredegund had been convinced the woman had betrayed Clovis with her seduction, but she was no longer certain. If the woman survived, Fredegund may well let her head remain attached.

As the crowd closest to Clovis pushed and scrambled to move beyond the range of his flames, the first wave of lower echelon grotesques dived in to flame around the outer edge of the square. With nowhere to go, the throng of humans crushed in on itself in terror.

Just as Fredegund began to think their attack would end in a rout there was a loud whump followed by a scream of agony. Horrified, she watched a grotesque tumble to the ground.

The Horde had been prepared. Only now did Fredegund notice the temporary shelters on top of several of the buildings around the square. Covers were thrown back to reveal soldiers firing large harpoons from strange metal machines. The machines swivelled in all directions, picking off the grotesques flying within the square one-by-one.

One of the machines swung its barrel up until its muzzle angled towards where she and the remaining males hovered. They scattered. The flurry of harpoons reached their former position with unprecedented reach, speed and precision.

Audon shouted, "I'll burn them."

"No, Audon. Wait." Fredegund's retort came too late.

The Queen's consort already had his wings tucked in tight and was plunging towards the machine. The human soldiers took aim but didn't survive to fire. They were swarmed by the putti.

The cherubic devils swept over the machines and the soldiers arming them. They grabbed handfuls of hair, tugged their victims off their feet, and tossed them from the rooftops with child-like glee. The putti followed the soldiers over the edges.

Audon swept by, blasting the machines with fire so hot their frames buckled and warped. The battle had swung back in favour of the grotesques.

The sight of soldiers being flung into the air turned the humans against one another in their desperation to escape. Fredegund waited for them to inflict maximum damage on themselves before she signalled the remaining grotesques to take up their attack once more. They swooped.

The putti withdrew into the alleyways, far enough to be safe, close enough to profit from the impending feast of flesh. Their demure rose-bud lips split into wide grins exposing rows of pointed teeth that would soon tear flesh from bone.

The grotesques pitched into the square in two waves. The first group swept around fast, blasting a wall of fire over the swirling crush of humans. The second wave dropped lower and burned any who survived. The only humans remaining alive in the square were those too close to Clovis and the woman held safe within his wings. The lower echelons of the grotesques landed and arranged themselves to prevent any human reinforcements from entering the square.

Fredegund, not part of the fiery attack, dropped into the square. She watched the putti flock in to tear through blackened skin into raw bloody flesh and noted with satisfaction that not one touched the fallen grotesques.

"GUARDIAN."

Her head snapped around at Clovis' scream. The pyre was engulfed in flames, which already writhed around his legs. A group of human males stood nearby. The one dressed in the shiny blue robe held a burning torch in his hand. The others surrounded the man in blue with their shields held high and swords drawn. She would deal with them soon.

Audon had also heard the yell and leaped over the mounds of charred flesh to reach Clovis first. Together she and Audon tore at the iron bonds, trying to prise them apart with their bare hands.

"Save the Charm." Clovis flung the human woman high in the air, clear of the flames.

Audon flipped and twisted to catch the human woman. Despite her screams and struggle, he lifted her away.

Clovis was burning. "Remove my head, Guardian." His eyes bore into hers. "I beg of you Fredegund, spare me this agony."

It was a ridiculous moment to feel joy, but she did. He'd used her name.

A long-knife flashed silver-blue and the head of Clovis dropped into her arms. Beaten back by the flames, she watched his body slump against its bonds. The skin cracked and blackened. His limbs twisted in a macabre dance until the raging fire consumed him.

Within her arms the head, deprived of life-giving blood, began to transform. It hardened and changed until the eyes staring back at her were dark grey stone. His face frozen in an eternal grimace, large lips stretched wide over fanged teeth.

Audon landed and placed the now silent woman on her feet. Fredegund stared into the face of the woman for whom Clovis had chosen to sacrifice his life. Reddened eyes stared back at her from eye sockets streaked with garish colours and smudges of black. The woman's hair hung in a tangled mess, the fabric of her covering singed and blackened by fire. Yet she held herself tall, chin lifted in confidence.

Of all the grotesques, the Guardian had come face to face with the most humans over the centuries. Never had she observed one who emanated such subtle power. Could this have been what Clovis sensed?

"I am Martha, the Charm." The woman stretched out her hand to touch the stone head still nestled in Fredegund's arms. "May I look into his face once more?"

"I am Fredegund, the Guardian." She crouched and turned the head in her hands so Martha could stare down into Clovis' stone eyes.

• • • •

Martha's fingers traced the contours of the petrified face of her fallen lover in silence, then she leaned forward to kiss him once more. The chill from his stone lips pierced her soul and stabbed at her heart. Her own face hardened. She tightened her grip on the soldier's sword still clutched in her hand.

"Fredegund, his killer is mine. I will have my revenge."

A fierce smirk contorted the Guardian's face. She bared her fangs. "He is yours, Martha the Charm. All I ask is that you do not damage his head."

Martha nodded.

Romanus stood within the protective cocoon of overlapping shields held by his personal guards. They were trapped at the very centre of the square. Any escape to the safety of the tower not only blocked by the grotesques prowling the square, but also by the morass of bodies, and the voracious putti who devoured them.

"Romanus. I promised you death and here I am. Come, face me," said Martha.

He laughed. "You will not kill me, Charm. I am your Lord, the one who blooded you, who gratified you. It was I who created you from nothing. You are mine."

"You may have blooded the innocent Martha, but you, my Lord, failed in your efforts to gratify the Charm. She found no pleasure in your touch, only disgust. It took one much nobler than yourself to provide the pleasure she craved and needed to fulfil her destiny."

"Lying bitch. I gave you pleasure. I filled your filthy cunt with it."

"You know nothing of pleasure. It was Clovis who made me who I am when he flew me beneath the twin moons. I am Martha the Charm, and I will be mother to the Redeemer."

The guards gasped at her invocation of the forbidden legend. Romanus' face turned purple, and his eyes bulged. He pushed past the lowering ring of shields.

"I will kill you before I allow you to whelp an abomination, ungrateful whore." He pulled a jewelled dagger from the belt that hung on his hips and lunged.

Martha lifted the sword with two hands and spun aside, deflecting his furious attack. Romanus stumbled but recovered his footing. He stabbed at her from the side. Martha gasped when his blade sliced the flesh of the forearm flung up to protect herself. The heavy sword fell with a clatter to the paving stones. Injured and disarmed, she staggered away, before he could press his advantage.

"Catch." It was Fredegund.

Martha glimpsed a silvery-blue flash from the corner of her eye and reached out in reflex. Her fingers closed around the hilt of a long-knife. It felt familiar in her grip, as though she had wielded it for a thousand years.

Romanus moved towards her. She watched his face grimace in exertion and his eyes narrow with hate. His pretty knife plunged towards her heart. The red covering swirled away from her body as she pirouetted on one foot, arm extended at shoulder height. The blade sliced through skin, flesh and bone without effort.

The cleaved head rolled to land between Fredegund's feet. The Guardian roared with laughter and pissed on it in final insult. Romanus' headless body stayed upright for two heartbeats before it succumbed to gravity and the onslaught of half a dozen putti.

Martha swayed, then tumbled into the void.

• • • •

At the fall of Romanus, his guards fell to their knees and begged for their lives.

"You see what happens when you, the Horde, challenge the order of our world?" Fredegund swept her arm at the devastation around them. "You not only bring great suffering and loss upon others, but also upon yourselves. Go now. Return to your people and prepare them. For all is changed, the cycle is broken and only time will tell what horrors the Redeemer will bring to the world."

Abandoning their swords and shields, the guards turned and picked their way through the tangle of burnt and twisted flesh. They entered the safety of the tower without a further glance behind them.

Martha the Charm, bearer of the Redeemer, lay safe in Audon's arms. He held her limp body with great care. Fredegund had never imagined the Redeemer would come in her lifetime. It would change everything. The Guardian's life would, from this day forth, be dedicated to the care and protection of the woman.

"Take her to the Queen and explain what has happened. Mother will know how to bring the Charm back from her darkness."

Without waiting for Audon to leave, Fredegund waved over Merovech.

"I am pleased you survived, Merovech. I need you to organise our fallen to be taken to the Chateau. Then, you and the others must feed before tonight."

"Guardian, I am not of the upper echelon and am not worthy of this task. I will fetch another over for your orders."

"Merovech, I have chosen you. The cycle is broken. The petty hierarchies of our clan no longer count for anything. Do my bidding. The putti and I will finish our work here. I will return and join you when the pink moon follows the silver above the horizon. Then we will lay our fallen to rest in the crypt. Now go."

She completed her grim task with methodical efficiency, the blue blades of her knives flashing in the afternoon sun. The putti gathered the heads in bundles knotted together by their hair, then carried them to the Chateau. Between flights, the putti continued to gorge on human flesh. Some were already changing – their bodies slimmer, limbs longer and facial features less child-like.

The sun slid low on the horizon and the last of the putti took flight. Only two heads remained, sitting in the centre of the square where Fredegund had left them. She kicked the human head aside and crouched down in front of the other. She lifted the head of Clovis with great reverence and rose into the air.

At the top of the human tower, she positioned the petrified head against the smooth stone wall, so it gazed upon the square and across the plain to the Chateau. With precise blasts of white fire, she melted stone into stone. Clovis would be a permanent feature of the human structure, a constant reminder of the destruction the Horde bought upon themselves. She dropped into the city square for the final time.

With a wicked giggle, Fredegund pissed on the human head again, then snatched it up by its hair. She vaulted into the air and followed the last of the sun's rays back to the Chateau.

Soaring over the walls of the keep, she tossed the head away. The slain leader of the Horde had no right to have his skull preserved in the hall. That location was reserved for the heads of respected adversaries who lost their lives to the grotesques with honour. The head tumbled to smash on the flagstones of the courtyard. A gang of the sweet-faced putti who'd been too small to fly to the human city descended on the splattered remains with gusto.

The silver moon crested the far horizon. If Fredegund hurried she would arrive in the crypt in time to assist with the interment of the fallen. Landing at the far side of the courtyard, she ran through the archway over the entry to the stone staircase. She took the steps three at a time, spiralling into the gloom and dust far below.

The ritual was short and silent – the dead could no longer hear them, and no words could bring them back to life. They laid the stone corpses where space allowed. In time, like their ancestors before them, their features would soften as they capitulated to mould and lichen. The living did not linger.

Back in the early-evening light of the waning moons the grotesques stretched their wings in flight, celebrating their victory and survival. The males dipped and swerved around each other in mock battles. They were joined by the eight newest grotesques, the matured putti.

Fredegund crouched alone atop the tallest tower. She watched the putti gather on the crest of the hall roof. They wrestled and giggled with the innocence of the young. Then took up the positions they would occupy for the years until the Redeemer called upon them.

All too soon the silver moon was overhead, and the grotesques flew down to their perches. With the losses and new arrivals, it took time to settle. Audon was the last to take his place. He looked at her.

"I never dreamed I would hold this position, Fredegund," he said.

"Audon, you are both intelligent and brave, and have shown that physical strength is not always necessary to win. I believe you, and only you, can provide the leadership we will need when you awaken in our new world. I am honoured to be your Guardian."

Then, Audon did what had never been done. He flew the Guardian.

Fredegund thought her heart would burst. She, who had cared for others for more than a millennium, now knew ecstasy on the wing. At last, she understood the rapture of the Queen. But the experience was bitter-sweet. Once the flight finished, all except her returned to stone. She was alone.

Alone, except for her mother, and Martha the Charm.

• • • •

Martha awoke in unfamiliar surroundings. She lay in an enormous bed snuggled deep beneath an eiderdown both light and cosy. Stretching to release the sleep from her limbs she felt the tug of the moons. The Charm stirred within her, yearning for his touch, only to retreat as memories of the day's horrors flooded her mind. Martha curled, foetal-like, body shuddering in pain.

The night had grown deeper the next time she awoke. The room was enormous. Mauve fingers of moonlight penetrated the gloom through large windows and a pair of open doors. Climbing from the bed, she stepped through the doors onto an enclosed balcony. After the warmth of the bed, she shivered at the chill of the night air.

She was high in one of the towers of the Chateau. Looking around she could see the frozen forms of the putti arranged around the roof edge below. In the distance, the lights of the city she had called home glimmered through a misty pall.

"We brought you here."

Martha screamed and tripped as she spun in the direction of the voice. A thick tail cushioned her fall.

"I did not mean to frighten you. I am Brunhilda, Queen and mother to the grotesques."

Brunhilda stepped down from the gloom of her perch on the balustrade and into the moonlight, a musky odour wafting before her. The Charm filled Martha with a desire to bury herself within the Queen's ample folds.

"You surprised me, that is all." Martha scrambled to her feet. She looked up to be confronted by the intense green-eyed stare of the Queen crouched before her. Heart pounding, she dipped her head in respect. "Majesty, I thank you for bringing me here to safety."

"I did not understand how Clovis could have fallen under your spell, when he had me, his Queen and lover, awaiting his victory," Brundhilde rumbled. "But now I see it was not the human, Martha, he saw...no, not Martha at all. Clovis fell for the Charm." Her massive hand reached out to rest on Martha's belly. "He impregnated you under the power of the twin moons. You are the bearer of the Redeemer."

The Charm quivered with a delight Martha also felt. She lay her own small hand over the Queen's.

"I confess, Queen Brunhilda, I am afraid of the future. Where will I go? What will I do?"

"Do not be afraid. You will stay here. Fredegund will protect and care for you."

"Fredegund?" Emboldened by the Queen's scent, she stepped closer. "Not yourself?" Martha climbed into Brunhilda's embrace, reaching up to run her tongue across luscious lips. She moaned. Their tongues engaged in a delicious skirmish.

Brunhilda sighed and broke from Martha's clasp. "Oh, you are a tempting delight my dear, but the cycle is broken, and I am unable to surrender to your offerings. I have not been flown and, my wombs are empty. I will enter the long slumber of stone before the pink moon begins its descent."

Martha the Charm could not keep the disappointment from her face.

"Do not look like that, my little one. Like you, my daughter Fredegund was bred for her role and is exceptional in her talents. She will be devoted to you. I promise, you will be safe with her here."

Without another word Brunhilda disappeared off the balcony into the night. Alone again, Martha once more felt the chill of the night air and retreated to the warmth of the bed.

• • • •

The Charm had been created by the human Horde to weaken their winged foe. However, the human architects of her design had not figured Martha into their alchemy of grotesque blood pumping through human flesh. Martha, who despite the training and deprivations of her upbringing, had her own thoughts, desires and feelings.

The Horde, intent on retaining their adopted world, had created a weapon to destroy what they feared the most. Instead, they had created the weapon of their own ultimate destruction.

About the Author

Jacqui has lived an adventure-filled life, spanning a range of careers and countries. She's wrangled kindergarten children, driven buses, researched humpback whales, spoken at the United Nations, visited Antarctica, and farmed deer. These days she writes strange and sometimes sexy fiction. Jacqui doesn't believe in happily ever after, so shares her house with a cat.

Read more at www.jacquigreaves-author.com.

Milton Keynes UK
Ingram Content Group UK Ltd.
UKHW010724200923
429044UK00001B/36